NIGHT WITH A TIGER

ALASKAN TIGERS: BOOK FOUR

MARISSA DOBSON

Published by Dobson Ink
Printed in the United States of America
ISBN-13: 978-1-939978-25-7

Dedication

To Thomas—my wonderful husband who's been supportive through everything. He's put up with my late night writing sessions, cooked dinner, over all he's been wonderful. Thank you Thomas.

To my readers who love the Alaskan Tigers as much as I enjoy writing them. Enjoy this newest adventure to Alaska.

Chapter One

With the precision of years of experience behind the helm, Adam Merks landed the helicopter. The private landing strip, just south of Dallas, Texas, was quiet. The only sound he heard as he stepped onto the grass was the rustle of leaves and the chirps of birds in the distance. His rented four-by-four pickup truck was parked twenty feet ahead, shining like a black diamond in the evening sun. It seemed too clean and new for where he was going. It would make him stand out, but this vehicle was the best Connor could do on such short notice.

Anxious to begin his search for Robin Zimmer, he tugged his small duffle bag from the helicopter and headed to the truck. With a little luck on his side, he'd be able to seek out Robin before night fell on the sleepy little town she was holed up in this week.

Slinging his duffle bag over his shoulder, he jogged toward the truck desperate to get out of the sweltering sun. After living in Alaska for years, he wasn't used to the heat, especially not this type in April. He held no desire to spend any unnecessary time here. The sooner he found Robin and convinced her he only wanted to help, the quicker he could return to Alaska and the cool spring weather.

Opening the driver's door, he found a pair of black cowboy boots and matching hat. Just the right outfit he needed to fit in at Royalwood. Tossing his bag onto the passenger's seat, he leaned against the truck and unlaced his black steel-toe boots. All Alaskan Tigers guards wore these boots for traction in the Alaskan snow. He slipped on the cowboy boots and wiggled his toes inside, trying to get used to the feel of the pointed toe. He then reached in the cab for the cowboy hat before a quick glace in the side mirror at his reflection. Adam was stunned. The hat made him look the part, but now he had to blend in and appear to be just another southern boy passing through. In a small town like Royalwood, he would also have to act the part for people to look passed him.

Ready to get the day moving, he jumped into the pickup and started the engine, desperate to get the air conditioning on to cool down the sweltering heat filling the truck. With the cool air circulating, he unclipped his cell phone from his belt. Sliding his finger over the screen to unlock it, he sent Ty a text message. *Arrived and on my way to Royalwood. I'll be in touch once I make contact with Robin.*

He dropped the phone into the cup holder and shifted the truck in Drive. Determination ran through him. If there was any hope to save Tabitha and all of the tiger shifters, he had to find Robin before Pierce and his gang of rogues. She held a key to Pierce's organization, and it was Adam's job to find out what it was.

Robin Zimmer stood outside the small café, soaking up the warm sun shining through the trees, debating her next move. The problem of finding a job in a small town was near impossible, and if she didn't find something soon, she'd have to move on. Royalwood, Texas was supposed to be her chance to add funds to her stash before moving on again. Running from Pierce and his men began to take its toll, not only on her bank account, but also on her state of mind.

She wasn't sure how much longer she could handle life on the run, and was eager to end this cross-country marathon. She rolled her stiff shoulders.

Maybe I should give myself up? Could what Pierce had in store for her be any worse than what she was already doing to her exhausted body? When she ran as far as she could from Virginia, she considered the option, but surrendering to Pierce meant her ultimate death. *Would that be such a bad thing?* She shook the disheartening thought from her mind. *Damn. There's got to be a way out of this. I just have to get some food and time to think.*

Strolling down the deserted street, she made her way to the family restaurant across from the hotel. Robin cursed again. She had no plan when she ran, only packing clothes for cold weather. Since it had been late February, and cold, winter still sank its claws into the residents. In Texas there was no winter, not like in Virginia. It was now early April and close to eighty degrees, completely unsuitable for long sleeves, but her budget wouldn't extend to purchasing new clothes. Two months on the run and she was exhausted.

This might be the last hot meal she'd enjoy if she couldn't find a job. The bag of chips and cold sandwich she had picked up at the gas station just didn't cut it day after day. Her finances weighed heavily on her mind for the first time in her life. Only eight weeks ago, she had a position in one of the leading law firms, without even a trace of a worry where money was concerned. Now her world was completely turned upside down. Pushing open the restaurants door, she let the coolness of the air conditioning wash over her, and enjoyed a moment of calming.

"Hey sweetie, sit wherever you'd like." An older woman, with a little extra around the middle and gray sprinkling through her otherwise chestnut, short hair, called to Robin from behind the counter.

"Thanks." Walking to the furthest table where she could watch the street and still have her back against a wall, her gaze fell over the few people in the restaurant. To determine if they might be the ones trailing her, she visually searched them for clues. On the run, she had no choice but to be cautious, to question every person's intentions. Her life depended on knowing who was around her and where the nearest exits were.

Satisfied that no one seemed dangerous, and an emergency exit to her right, she settled onto the hard, wooden chair and opened the menu. Even over the top of the menu, her gaze watched everyone. No one appeared suspicious, but still she couldn't relax. The hairs on the back of her neck stood up. She sensed something coming. During her time running from town to town she had learned to trust her body's instincts. Gut reactions had saved her more then once.

The waitress that welcomed her, eased up to the table. "So, what can I get you?"

"Umm…I'll take the special, to go. Please." Robin wiped her sweaty hands on her jeans. She knew, without a doubt, she had to get back to her hotel room. Maybe even out of town.

"Sure thing, just hang tight. I'll get you the meatloaf special, but you'd enjoy it better if you ate it while it's hot." The waitress jotted down the order on her notepad.

"Thanks, but I'm in a hurry today." She pulled out the money for the meal and handed it to the older woman. "If you could rush it, I'd appreciate it." To get the message of her hastiness across, she added a little extra to the woman's tip.

The bonus served to work just as Robin planned. Within a few minutes, she was crossing the quiet street to her stuffy hotel room, the hot food in her hand. Taking a quick glance around the parking lot as she made her away to her door, one new addition caught her gaze. A shiny, black truck with an extended cab that seemed out of place. Royalwood was a small farming community; no one here owned a brand new truck. This town was off the beaten path, enough that it was unlikely a businessman would be passing through. *It's time for me to move on. Someone or something is coming, and I don't want to be here when it arrives.* Speeding her pace, she sprinted to her door. The need to get inside and out of the open was overwhelming.

Once darkness fell, she'd slip into her car and drive out of town as fast as she could. Not expecting to move on before she had time to gather a little money, she didn't have her next destination in mind yet, but she'd find somewhere and try again. What choice did she have?

Keeping close to the buildings lining the street, she stayed in the shadows in case anyone was watching. She finally reached her room. She balanced her takeout container and drink in one hand, and slipped the key into the lock with the other. Boots clicked on the concrete sidewalk, coming toward her, as the lock slid home, it was too late. Taking a deep breath, she pretended to be just another traveler entering a hotel room, but no matter how hard she tried, she couldn't suppress the fear pounding in her chest.

Fear stinks to a shifter, more than any other emotion. Those were the last words her husband said to her before he died. *Damn him! If it wasn't for him, I wouldn't be running across the country, scared they'll find and kill me.*

"Ma'am…"

The man tipped the rim of his cowboy hat, giving her a glimpse of the greenest eyes she had ever seen. They reminded her of wet grass after a heavy rain. Gripping the door handle, she eased the door open, wishing she could step inside and find the safety she craved, but if this man was a shifter, the thin, wood door would do nothing to stop him from getting her. She forced a smile, and backed into the room. She made an attempt to slam the door, but a large boot stopped the speed of her effort.

"Don't be afraid, I'm here to help." He stepped toward her, forcing her further into the room.

"Please…" Panic threatened to close her throat. Robin swallowed the lump and backed away from the stranger. "Please, I don't want to die."

Stepping into the small room, he shut the door and then shoved the curtain aside to peek outside. "I said, I'm here to help. Why do you think I want to kill you?"

"You don't?" She couldn't hide the surprise from her voice. She sat the food on the dresser, not removing her stare from him. "If you're not here to kill me, then why are you here? What do you want? If it's money, I don't have much, but take it." She tossed her purse toward him.

He turned away from the window and grabbed the purse in the air. He laid it on the table. "I don't want your money, Robin. I've been sent to find you, to keep you safe. I know the people who are after you and the situation behind your disappearance. I understand it's a lot to ask, but you need to trust me because if not things are going to get hairy fast. There's been a shifter here—outside your door within the last few hours. It might not be the people after you, either way I'd rather err on the side of caution and ask you to come with me, to somewhere safer."

"How am I supposed to trust you? How do I know you're not with them, trying to lure me out of Royalwood to kill me?" She wished she had put her husband's gun in her purse. *Damn! A gun's not going to be any use in the suitcase.* It could have been the one thing that saved her if the situation got out of hand. It wouldn't kill a shifter, but it might give her time to escape, if not she could hope it would piss him off enough to kill her quickly.

"I realize trust at this point is difficult. It wasn't long ago that I was put into a similar position that you find yourself in. I was given a choice, which I chose to trust. If you want to save your life, you'll do the same." As he advanced toward her, she scurried to the side of the bed. He didn't let the bed stop him, stepping around it to stand in front of her. "Tabitha, the Queen of the Tigers and my Alpha's mate, feared you would not see the helping hand before you and reject it out of fear. I'm telling you the truth. I know your husband tried to trade your life for his own, and he was still killed and now they're after you. We must act quickly. Is there anything I can do to prove my intentions are true to you?"

"Why do we have to leave so quickly?" She was against the wall, unable to go any further. If he wanted to kill her, he was close enough to do it, and there was nothing she could do to stop him. She was no match to a shifter.

"If whoever was here earlier returns, they'll smell my scent. Pierce would have sent a team, if not more, to find you. I'm alone. I can't fight the rogues and protect you at the same time. Please, grab your things. I'll explain everything once you're somewhere safe."

"I don't need you. I've stayed alive this long and I can continue until they give up." It pained her to turn down help, but to trust him might lead her to an early grave.

"You're doing a great job, going from town to town, hiding in a different hotel room. Is that truly how you want to live?" He grabbed her small, wheeled suitcase from the side of the wall and tossed it on the bed. "If you want to reclaim your life, gather your stuff. I'm leaving in ten minutes. Be ready if you're coming with me."

"Are they really here?" Her stomach turned at the thought that if this stranger hadn't shown up, she might not have been able to escape before the rogues returned and found her.

"Yes, I believe the scent I caught is from one of the rogues." He walked to the window. "Nine minutes."

Do I trust him? She wrapped her arms around her stomach, hugging her body. *What do I have to lose?* If he was here to kill me, I'd be dead already, and if the rogues were close, she didn't stand a chance. If she wanted to live, then this man was her only chance.

Chapter Two

Adam drove the truck onto the highway, racing back to Dallas. He had already called and made reservations at Manetka Resort, a hotel owned by the Alpha of the Texas Tigers, Avery. This resort catered to the shifters traveling through the area. Manetka, the Polish word for shifter, was a safe haven for their kind. Adam would have them there in twenty minutes and then he'd explain everything to Robin. With luck on his side, they'd fly out at first light.

"Who are you?" Robin sat squished up against the passenger door, her hand resting on the door handle as if she was preparing to jump out at any second, which wouldn't be a good decision on her part while he was doing seventy miles an hour down the freeway.

"I should have done a proper introduction before, but getting you to safety took priority. I'm, Adam Merks, from the Alaskan Tiger's clan. For weeks we've been searching for you."

"We've?"

He shot her a quick glance. Fear clearly filled her beautiful eyes. "My clan. We've been after Pierce and his gangs of rogues, and because of that search, we found information about you. Our computer expert, Connor, has been following your trail across the country. Yesterday he finally caught up to you, which is why I'm here."

"Why…why would you care if they're after me?

He checked his blind spot, before guiding the truck into the next lane and then put his foot down on the accelerator. In his rear view mirror, he saw a truck weaving in and out of the traffic, quickly approaching. "Shit."

"What?" Panic rose in her voice, as she followed his stare.

"There's a green truck coming up behind us. We need to lose it, before they follow us to Manetka Resort."

"This isn't going to end until I'm dead." The terror seemed to be lost from her words, replaced by unmistakable sadness.

"I'll keep you safe." Adam needed to get off the main road. He cut across the traffic at the last minute to catch an exit, which led into a small town. Turning onto one of the side streets, he unclipped his cell phone from his belt and pressed a button before putting the phone to his ear.

"Did you make contact?" Ty asked.

"Yes, sir. Robin is with me. We were on our way to Manetka, but they spotted us. I need Connor to find me a rental that's open late. I have to swap this truck before they find us again."

"I'll get him on it right away. Just hang tight for a few minutes." Adam heard mumbled words that he was unable to make out. Ty returned moments later. "Instead of going to Manetka, can you come back here?"

"I'll see what I can do, but I haven't had time to tell Robin anything yet. Someone was lurking around her hotel room shortly before I arrived. I convinced her to come with me, but I'm not sure she will join me in the helicopter without an explanation first." Adam paused, glancing at Robin who was frowning at him. "She's exhausted from being on the run, and she's in need of a hot meal and a good night sleep."

"Okay, keep us updated. Connor is sending you the coordinates to the rental company now. They're expecting you." Ty paused for a moment, sighing into the phone. "Tell Robin why you went to find her. If she knows we want to take down the man that killed her husband, she might cooperate quicker."

"Thanks, Ty. Could you make contact with Avery and have someone he trusts keep an eye on the helicopter? I doubt the rogues found it, but if I can convince Robin to leave tonight, I want to make sure we're not walking into an ambush."

"Good point. I'll see to it."

Adam shoved the phone in his shirt pocket.

"Helicopter? To go where? Tell me what's going on?" She gripped the dashboard as she bombarded him with questions.

Adam programmed Connor's coordinates into the truck's GPS. "I told you, I'm from Alaska. I flew in this afternoon to find you and bring you to our compound—to safety." With the GPS set, he glanced at her. "Is it safe to assume you're not willing to fly out with me now? I can explain everything on the way. We could at least leave Dallas and go to another location before going to Alaska."

"I don't know. What are you *not* telling me?" She turned in her seat, pushing back against the door and stared out the back window.

He drove the truck further into the town, away from the highway, and hopefully further away from the rogues chasing them. "The rental company is just down the road. To explain everything is going to take longer than the drive. I'll change the truck, and then we'll talk. Okay?" He wanted to pull to the side of the road and tell her everything she wanted to know, but that would give the rogues a chance to catch up to them.

Fifteen minutes later, they were in a different truck and heading around the outskirts of Dallas. Robin wasn't sure if they were going to the helicopter or to the resort. Trusting the man that sat beside her, seemed risky, but no more than facing the world alone again. She was tired of being alone, and tired of running. If trusting Adam could get her out of this life threatening situation, then she would.

The town lights drifted away, leaving only darkness outside the truck's windows. "So what aren't you telling me?"

He drove the truck into a small turn-around on the side of the road, and put it in park before turning toward her. "We've been hunting Pierce for some time now. He's also the man searching for you. Years ago, he murdered Tabitha's parents, and he's recently added to his kill list. Bethany's parents and her sister were Pierce's latest victims. Tabitha sent me to find you, so you don't end up as another life lost to Pierce's madness."

"Who's Bethany?"

"She's the mate of the clans Lieutenant, Raja. Her family was targeted because Pierce feels they're partially responsible for him being a weretiger." He paused as car lights came toward them. He watched the vehicle in the side mirror until it passed.

"Weretiger? I thought those who were two-natured preferred to be called shifters."

Adam's gaze left the road to focus on her. "They do. Shifters are born, and weres are bitten. It's rare and only happens because of rogues. Weres can only change during a full moon. They are extremely unstable and close to rogues. Bethany's uncle married a woman who suffered with a mental illness that was passed onto her son. As a teenager he turned rogue, and bit Pierce."

"But why have I been dragged into all of this? I didn't even know about shifters until they killed my husband." That wasn't completely true, but it was the first time she had contact with them. She fiddled nervously with a lose button on the sleeve of her shirt. "I just want my life back."

Adam slipped his cowboy hat off and tossed it on the dashboard before turning to her once again. His sparkling, green eyes met her gaze. "Pierce won't stop until you're dead. We'd prefer to get him first. You have to trust me. I'll keep you safe, Robin. You just need to come back to Alaska with me. Once you are safe, we can take down Pierce without worrying that one of his rogues is still searching for you."

She shook her head with such determination; a strand of her long, curly brown hair fell from its clip. "I haven't trusted a soul in longer than I can remember. Trust has always led to heartache and trouble. It's part of the reason I'm in this shitty situation."

"Excuse me for being frank, but your late husband was scum. Offering you to the rogues to save his own skin is one of the worst things a man can do. Even with his barter, they still killed him, and you…had you not ran, your death would have been torturous. He'd have tortured you before killing you, just for sport. Now he only wants to see you eliminated. Pierce fears your husband told you something important. He'll keep you running until he eliminates you. As long as you're alone and on the run, you can't tell anyone those secrets."

She stared into his eyes, wishing she could fall into them. The green of his eyes reminded her of walking through a prosperous meadow, the sun on her skin, and the wind in her hair. No worries weighed down her shoulders as she gazed into those dreamy eyes. "I don't know anything. Maybe if he knew that, he'd let me live."

"If only it could be that easy. Pierce is a rogue, he doesn't think along the same lines as sane people do. He won't believe you. He'll think you're lying, which will only piss him off more."

"Then how can you help me?"

"My clan has been after him for some time now and we're closing in on him. Until then, you'll be safe in Alaska. There are guards around the perimeter to keep everyone safe. I understand it's not the life you had, but it has to be better than running from town to town, looking over your shoulder. Once Piece has been terminated, then you can decide what you want to do." Adam's phone vibrated in his pocket, drawing his attention. "It's a text from my Alpha."

While he checked his text message, she pondered her options. *I want to go back to Virginia and gather the pieces that were once my life, not follow this man to Alaska. Damn you, Bobby. That bastard died, but not before he made sure my life was a living hell.* With her car back at the hotel, and money running thin, she didn't have much choice but to trust Adam.

He tossed his cell phone into the cup holder. "One of the Texas Tigers is guarding the helicopter. There's no sign that anyone has found it. I hate to rush your decision, but if we want to get out here before they find the landing strip, we have to leave soon."

"Is there anything else you're not telling me?" She knew he hadn't told her everything. It was the way he chose his words, with the extra care, as if watching his words carefully.

"Yes. Ty has given me permission to tell you everything, in order for you to make your decision."

"What?" Disappointment filled her. Would he have held back if she hadn't asked? "Tell me or I'm not going."

He turned, resting his arm along the back of the seat. He focused on her as if she was the only person left in the world. "Tabitha believes you're the key to finding Pierce."

"Why? Because he'll follow me to Alaska?"

"There's a book of old magic that's been assisting Tabitha on her journey. This book told her of you and your predicament. This information started our journey to find you. Without the book we wouldn't have known anything about you, or that Pierce was after you."

A book? This situation was getting more ridiculous by the minute.

Chapter Three

Relief flooded through Adam when Robin said two little words, *I'll go.* Now it was time to get the hell out of dodge before Pierce's rogues caught their scent again. Not wanting to risk someone seeing them in the city, Adam raced around the outskirts of Dallas, toward the helicopter waiting on the other side.

Robin sat passively next to him, her body curled in a tight ball, holding her knees against her chest, while she stared out the window. The stench of her fear filling the truck's interior, forced him to breathe through his mouth. The compassionate side of him wanted to relieve her fears. Anything he could have said only tasted like a lie. The cat in him wanted to play with her as if she was food. Tigers enjoyed the smell of fear from their prey, but Robin wasn't his prey, she was his mission—a target to keep out of the hands of the rogues. He wouldn't fail her. Too many souls had already fallen at the rogues' mercy, and Adam would make damn sure it wouldn't be Robin's fate.

"Alaska isn't as bad as most people think. Don't get me wrong, it's cold, but beautiful. My clan's originally from Pennsylvania so I understand the weather change from the East Coast. You'll be safe there. Let go of your fear and trust me. I won't let anything happen to you." His words probably mattered very little when her fear was overwhelming. He had to at least try.

"What do you know of fear?" The terror he could smell had turned her words to anger.

"More than most." Finding her in that crummy hotel room reminded him of his own experience of running from town to town, fearful for his life. Ty had found Adam when he thought he couldn't go on any longer. Months of running had left him without hope and seeing no option other than to end it all just to find a moment of peace. He may have ended his life if Ty hadn't stumbled upon him that night.

She turned away from the road, sadness clearly shadowing her face, and tears glistening in her eyes. "I'm sorry. I know my fear reeks to your type. I can't help it."

"I really do understand what you're going through. It's not going to be easy. Any information you give us might be the key to finding Pierce. Once he's eliminated you won't have to hide any longer, you can reclaim your life. Even if you don't want to accept it, you're part of the puzzle we need to defeat him."

"I'll do whatever is necessary to get my life back. I miss having a home, my job, friends, and all the little things I took for granted. For years, I was at Bobby's disposal—his toy and punching bag when he was angry, but no more. I want a life for me. I'm tired of living for someone else." She didn't bother to brush away the tears that now fell freely down her cheeks. It was almost as if she was embracing her freedom.

"I'll help you." He smiled. With traffic left behind them, he pushed down on the gas. "We'll be at the landing strip in five minutes."

"Good." Stifling a yawn, she turned back to the window.

"I'm sure you must be tired. You'll be able to sleep on the helicopter."

"I'm fine. My scattered nerves wouldn't let me sleep even if I wanted to."

The truck raced past a forest of trees with such speed they'd be at the landing strip sooner than he expected. "What are you nervous about? I'm not going to let anyone harm you. Are you concerned you're walking into a trap?"

"Why would you say trap?" Her fear raised several notches, nearly suffocating the air around him.

"Years ago, when I was in your position, I thought the same." He looked away from the road for a moment to study her face. "I can taste your anxiety on my tongue as if it was my own. Your apprehension isn't just for the ones you've been running from, you fear me as well."

Her lips curled into a frown, creasing her forehead with worry. "I won't deny it, because it would be like trying to tell you you're not truly a tiger. It would be pointless."

"Thank you." He was relieved she didn't try to refute the truth as most would. Rewarding her honesty, he wanted to share a secret with her. "If it makes you feel any better, your comfort is why I let you keep your gun."

"Gun?" She tried to act surprised, but her eyes betrayed her.

"I can smell gun powder. You have a small revolver in your purse." He winked. "I smelled it back at the hotel. I thought you'd feel safer with it, so I let you keep it." She gripped her purse, confirming his claims. "If you shoot me now, I'll never hear the end of it from my clan. My decision to let you keep it would shame me. Shifters heal from most gun shots, but they hurt like the dickens."

"I'm not going to shoot you. Damn it! I didn't think a shifter could smell it. At the hotel I was relieved when I was able to slip it out of my suitcase and into my purse without you noticing, but I guess it was a waste to sneak around if you can smell the gun powder."

He drove the truck onto a dirt road leading to the small deserted landing strip where the helicopter waited. He used only the parking lights to make the last trek through the dark woods to not draw any unnecessary attention. "There will be a member of the Texas Tigers clan waiting for us. While I meet with him, I want you to stay here. Just to be safe, I've shut off the dome light, that way when I open the door the cab won't illuminate. We don't know who or what could be lurking in the woods. Stay put, and keep your gun close. I'll be right back."

"Do you think they're here?"

Her fear tingled along his spine as he shifted the truck into park, stopping close to the helicopter. "No, safety is my main concern." Adam opened the door and stepped out of the truck. He glanced back at her to see her eyes wide, scanning the woods.

Tilting his head, he sniffed the air for any unfamiliar scents. All he caught was the tiger leaning against a car twenty paces away. Adam rolled his shoulders to relax his muscles, but kept his guard focused, listening and watching the surrounding dark woods. The sooner he could get Robin out of here, the better he'd feel.

"You must be Adam." The young tiger wore a creamy white cowboy hat that hid most of his blond hair. He couldn't have been older than twenty, yet his facial features resembled a man who had lived a long, hard life.

"Yes, and you are?"

"Tex." He accepted Adam's offered hand. "It doesn't look like anyone was here before I arrived and there hasn't been any movement since I took post."

Adam noticed that the skittish boy wouldn't make eye contact. "I appreciate you coming to stand guard…" Headlights lit up the trees to the left. "Shit." The road, the vehicle was travelling on, was the only way in or out here. With the helicopter not started and Robin still in the truck, he would have to stand ground against whoever was coming.

"Are they with you?" the boy asked.

Adam spotted two men in the front seat of the approaching car. "No, and I don't think they've just taken a wrong turn. Damn it!" He grabbed his gun from the holster, keeping it close to his side, hiding in the darkness until he was certain if danger was ahead. He didn't want to shoot an innocent tourist, or teenagers trying to find a place to make out.

"Avery doesn't allow anyone except his guards to carry weapons." Tex shrugged his shoulders.

"Hopefully you won't need one." Adam had a backup gun in his bag, as well as an additional knife strapped to his thigh, but there was no time to get either.

The car doors opened, shining the dome light onto the men in the car. Adam didn't know the passenger, but instantly recognized the dark haired driver as one of Pierce's men. *Shit.*

"Can I help you?" Adam watched the men as they stepped out of the car.

"Give us the woman and no one will get hurt." The driver pointed his weapon toward Adam. The safety clicked, echoing in the air.

"It's just us…" Tex started.

"We know she's here."

Adam fought the urge to glance at the truck, hoping Robin would stay hidden in the darkness. "You know I won't turn anyone over to you." He raised his gun, ready to shoot the driver. There was no discussion when it came to rogues, and quick action was his only chance to take out the opposition.

A shot rang out. Tex shifted to his animal form and lunged forward. It took Adam a split second to realize it was the passenger who shot, not the driver that Adam had his weapon trained on. He pulled the trigger, shooting the driver square between the eyes, killing him. It was the one shot that was fatal even to shifters. The wound couldn't heal if the brain was dead.

Tex scuffled with the other man on the ground. He was holding his own, but he was a young shifter and didn't stand a solid chance against the rogue.

The darkness prevented Adam from getting a clean shot. Another bang rang out, deafening him for a second as gunpowder filled his nose. *Tex!* He broke into an outright run. A roar of pain cut through the night air as Adam pulled the rogue away. Claws digging into Adam's side didn't stop him. He slammed the rogue into the cement with such force the rogue bounced. Using the heel of his cowboy boot, Adam placed his foot on the rogue's throat. He pressed hard, staring down at his enemy. "Where is Pierce?"

"I'll never tell you. Pierce will see your Alpha Female dead." His words were breathy, as he struggled under Adam's foot.

"That's where you're wrong. Pierce and his followers will never stand a chance. We will kill them long before they get near my Queen." Adam gripped his gun and shot the man. *Two more rogues down.*

Sliding the gun into his holster he ran toward Tex. The young tiger lay bleeding just beside the car. "Tex," Adam said, carefully approaching. An injured shifter would attack first and ask questions later if they felt threatened. Tex's eyes opened as he shifted back to his human form.

Lying naked on the ground, blood pooling around him from the wound to his abdomen, Tex reached for Adam's hand. "You have to help me…"

"It's okay. We'll get some help," Adam reassured him.

"No. Avery will see this as a failure. I'll be killed for not seeing you and your woman to safety."

"Tex, this was beyond your control. Avery knows there are rogues searching for her."

"It won't matter…" Tex's words were lost as his eyelids fluttered shut and he passed out.

He tore the end of his shirt and pressed it against Tex's wound. Adam then dashed to the truck. Coming around the front of the truck, he entered Robin's direct line of sight. He slowed his run, not wanting to frighten her more than she was. He didn't need an overemotional woman on his hands, especially if they were going to get off the landing strip before another batch of rogues found them.

Robin pushed the door open. "You're okay?" There was a touch of surprise in her tone.

"It takes more than two men with guns to take me down." He reached for their suitcases, and held out his hand. "We've got to go."

"What about the other tiger?"

"He's injured. Once I get you in the helicopter, I'll get him. I need the first aid kit from the copter anyway. Now come on, we don't have much time." She scooted to the edge of the seat and slid her hand into his. An electrical current coursed through him. She quickly pulled her hand away, her eyes wide with confusion.

"What was that?"

He debated for a moment to tell her what the electricity meant, but an explanation would take time they didn't have. "It's nothing."

"No! Tell me what that was or I'm not going anywhere with you." She stared at her hand almost as if expecting to see a burn.

"Robin, please." He glanced at Tex before turning back to her. "Once we're in the air I'll explain. Tex has been shot and I have to stop the bleeding. We have to get out of here. Other rogues will be coming." Adam had a suspicion that the rogue driver would have made a call when he spotted them. More rogues wouldn't be far behind.

Robin nodded, finally walking toward the helicopter. "Okay."

With Robin safely in the helicopter, Adam covered Tex with a blanket and laid him in the back. He tended to Tex's injuries with the few medical supplies he had, and then slid into the cockpit, starting the helicopter.

Robin sat beside him, her attention divided between watching the darkness and Tex. "Will he be all right?"

"Shifters can heal a wound like that, but he's not trying. He has to have the will to heal. I've done all I can for him. I have to get him back to Alaska, to our healers, if he's to stand any chance." The whoosh of the helicopter blades sliced the air as it picked up speed.

Lights flashed through the woods as another car entered the dirt road. "Shit." Glancing down at the gages, Adam hit a button, before turning to her. "Hold on. It might get rough if they start shooting." He pulled back on the lever, raising the helicopter from the ground.

Mates? Robin's thoughts were spinning with the insane thought of such a thing. Truthful to his word, after they were air born he explained the electrical touch she had experienced when she reached for his hand. Could the electrical current that passed through them in Texas really mean she was destined to be Adam's mate? It seemed like something out of a science fiction movie, not real life. She had enough of shifters to last a lifetime. She sure as hell didn't want one as a soul mate. For that matter, she didn't want any man, definitely not a shifter. Her husband, Bobby, had turned her off men forever.

The cooler Seattle air whipped through her hair, as Adam refilled the helicopter. Tex was still unconscious in the helicopter, but at least the bleeding had slowed. The bullet had gone straight through, leaving bleeding wounds on both sides, neither of which were healing as Adam had told her they should. Hopefully Tex would survive the last leg of their journey, and then the Alaskan Tigers healers could do their magic. Tex seemed to be struggling with something even as he lay unconscious. The pinched lines around his eyes and the soft moans were caused from more than just pain, fear shadowed both.

Adam's voice forced her out of her thoughts. "I didn't have a choice, there were more rogues. We barely escaped, Ty. He's only in his early twenties. I couldn't just leave him there to die." There was a pause as Adam clicked the fuel nozzle back on the holder. "Something's going on with Avery's clan, Ty. Tex has fresh wounds on his body, more than just training wounds, he's been abused." Adam nodded for her to get in, and then climbed on his seat, shutting his door. "Okay. We'll be there in a few hours, just have a healer ready." He ended the call and put his cell phone on his belt.

"Everything okay?"

"Yeah." He ran his hand over his five o'clock shadow. "I had to explain to my Alpha why I was bringing an injured shifter to our compound without the permission of his Alpha."

"You said Tex was abused, is that true? I thought they were friends of your clan? Are they rogues as well?"

"Most clans stick to themselves. The Alpha of the West Virginia Tigers, Jinx, is a close friend of ours and is currently at our compound. The Texas Tigers are different. They aren't rogues, but they have questionable practices. That will change in the future. Tabitha will unite all tiger shifters and there will no longer be separate practices as Avery has in Texas." Adam remained focused on the helicopter's instruments as he piloted out of Seattle.

"You didn't answer my question. Was he abused?" She glanced over her shoulder at the unconscious tiger. Sorrow filled her heart when she spotted scars marring his body.

"I believe so. Before he slipped into unconsciousness, he was scared of the consequences he'd receive at not protecting us. His fear makes me believe Avery might have killed him."

"What will happen to him?" She shook her head, looking away from Tex and back to Adam.

"That will be up to him. He could stay in Alaska and become a part of my clan or return to Texas, to Avery. He could also choose another clan or a life of solitude. He's young, so whatever choice he makes he can still have a life where his past won't haunt him."

"Unless he goes back to Avery."

"Yes." Adam nodded."

She didn't understand how Adam could sit idly by and let someone return to the person responsible for abuse. If someone had helped her get away from Bobby, she'd have left long before his death. Abusers hold power over those they mistreat, making them feel as if they'd never make it on their own. If Robin had a chance, she'd talk to Tex when he woke, and explain to him that he could have a life without violence.

Chapter Four

Being the second in command to Tabitha's guards, Adam had certain privileges. One was his own cabin, close to the main building. Landing the helicopter, he couldn't wait to sink onto his comfortable bed for a few hours of sleep. It had been over twenty-four hours since he had slept. Traveling through the night had been the final brick on the wall of his sleep deprivation.

"We're here." Stifling a yawn, he slipped the headset off and placed it on a hook above his head. In the dim morning light, he saw Ty and Raja standing off to the right. Galen, the healer, was a couple steps behind them.

With the helicopter blades coming to a stop, Robin whispered, almost as if she was afraid of the answer. "Now what?"

"You'll get some rest, and then we'll meet with the Elders in a few hours." The fear he smelled from her earlier had dissipated over the last few hours, but had returned with a vengeance, making the air heavy and hard to breathe. "I'll be with you. There's nothing to worry about, Robin. The Elders sent me to find you. They mean you no harm."

As Ty neared the helicopter, her anxiety raced off the chart, tearing through Adam as if the emotions were his own. He reached toward her, wanting to give her comfort—to do something to ease her fears. Slipping his hand over her small, clammy hand, the electricity sizzled through him. The current wasn't as strong because her rising panic overpowered the mating desire.

She shook her head. "I can't…"

"It's going to be all right." He circled the back of her hand with his thumb.

Her gaze went from him to the Elders that were approaching, and back to him. "Don't leave me…please."

"Okay. Just wait here for a moment. Let me talk to the Elders and then I'll take you to a cabin where you can get some sleep." He squeezed her hand before jumping out of the cockpit.

"How's she doing?" Ty shook Adam's hand.

Adam forced a smiled. "During the flight, I was able to relive most of her fears, but now that we've landed, she's freaking out. I suggest letting her get some sleep before questioning her."

"You both need rest. We've prepared the guest cabin next to yours for Robin. We'll speak with her later this afternoon."

"If it's okay, I think she'll be more comfortable in my cabin. She's scared, and I've established a trust with her." Adam glanced from Ty to Raja.

Raja took a deep breath, intensely watching Adam. "You've mated?"

"Not yet, but a connection is present. She's already in a weary state so I only explained the mating briefly. She's confused and she'll fight me with every step if I press it further right now." He ran his hand over his chin, feeling stubble beginning to grow. "Our mating is not why I want her in my cabin. She's been on the run for weeks. She feels safe with me and is beginning to trust me. If you want to question her, she'll need a sense of security. Being near me is going to provide her with that."

"Very well, and to show her we're a trusting clan, we'll come to your place to question her, to make it less formal. Say three o'clock?"

Adam nodded and turned to follow Galen to the helicopter, but Raja stopped him when he grabbed Adam's arm. "Avery is pissed that Tex didn't report back. We explained your situation with the rogues, so he's being patient for now, however he has requested Tex be returned by week's end."

"Will the boy have a choice? Or will he have to return to his abuser?"

"We will give Tex a choice, however it has to be his decision. You can't influence him or pressure his choice," Ty ordered.

Adam agreed, and then returned to assist Robin from the helicopter. He'd let the Elders deal with Tex. His attention was focused on Robin. Sliding the door open, he offered her his hand, and grabbed their suitcases. "Come on. Let's get some rest."

"What about your Elders?"

"We'll talk to them this afternoon. Now come on." He held her arm as she slipped out of the cockpit. Once she was safely on the ground, he slung his bag over his shoulder, laced his fingers through the handle of her suitcase, and wrapped his arm around her waist, leading the way to his cabin.

"I don't think I should be here," she whispered, gripping the sleeve of his shirt.

"No one here means you harm." He pulled her closer, letting her floral scent fill his nose. "I'll protect you."

Robin lay curled in a ball in the middle of the bed, her heart racing faster and faster with each second. Everything coming together at once sent her into full panic mode and was too much for her body to handle. Adam had gained her trust, but even knowing he was in the other room protecting her, she couldn't relax. Fear began to drown her.

"Robin," Adam whispered from the doorway, the sun streaming around him. "I know you're awake. Can I do anything for you? Get you anything?"

"I'm sorry I'm keeping you awake." Even to her own ears, her voice seemed strained.

"It's fine. I'm more worried about you." He moved away from the door, walking closer to the bed. "I can get Doc to give you something to help you relax."

"No!" His words sent a new wave of terror coursing through her.

"Shhh. I'm just trying to help. You're human, so your heart shouldn't be beating that fast. It's not safe. You have to calm down."

"I don't want any drugs."

"You don't have to. I only thought they would help you sleep. During your time on the run have you been filled with this much terror the whole time?" He stepped next to the bed. "Mind if I sit?"

She nodded. "I've never suffered from any type of panic attacks, until I was on the run. When my panic levels rise there's always been a reason. It's been like a sixth-sense, keeping me safe. But now...I don't know, this feels different." Her heart raced, beating against her chest with such power.

He reached out to her, gliding his fingers over her knuckles, before giving her hand a timid squeeze. "You're surrounded by shifters, the very race you've been running from, but I swear to you, you will come to no harm from my clan."

His touch seemed to calm her, slowing her heart rate, making her think it wouldn't fly out of her chest at any minute. "Why does your touch soothe me?"

"A touch from your mate will calm your emotions, ease your pain, and sometimes be a link for you to share thoughts. Tabitha can share her thoughts with Ty, and with concentration, even other members of the clan." He moved to rest his leg on the bed, brushing it along the curve of her body. "The more they touch, the closer they become, one calming the other."

"Relief." Her voice was husky. "Can you help me?"

"I'll lie down next to you, which may ease your stress."

"Anything. Please, just make this stop."

He let go of her hand and slid beside her. He lay on his back, swinging his arm above her to cuddle her into his body. The moment he settled, she slid close, snuggling next to him. Her panic instantly subsided, leaving her completely calm and at ease. "Ahhh."

"It feels good to have the worries fall away, doesn't it?" He ran his finger down her arm.

"Yes, but it won't last." Her eyes drifted shut as sleep wrapped its long tentacles around her, threatening to draw her under.

"It will, if you trust me." He turned her chin with the tip of his finger to force her to look at him. "I'm going to keep you safe."

She finally asked the question that had been weighing on her mind. "Because I might hold information that will help your clan?"

"That's why I was sent to find you. It's not why I protect you now. You're my mate and for that reason, I guarantee your safety." He nuzzled the top of her head.

"I'm not sure if I understand this whole mating thing."

Adam leaned back, meeting her gaze again. "I know, and I don't understand it completely either, but trust me. I would give my life for you."

She wasn't sure what to say to that, instead she closed her eyes. No longer tired, she lay there, letting her thoughts run wild with Adam's words. How was she supposed to act on this mating connection? She didn't want, or need, to be tied down to someone, especially a shifter. Everything she learned about shifters told her to stay away from them. Adam seemed different. She didn't want to create a distance from him, but she wasn't sure mating was for her.

Adam stood behind Robin, waiting for Ty to take the lead. His hands gently massaged her shoulder, trying to relieve some of her panic that returned. He hated to see her so full of conflicting emotions. Leaning, he whispered in her ear. "It's going to be all right."

Felix opened the door, ushering Tabitha in. "Sorry we're late. One of the young tigresses had an issue I needed to attend to." Tabitha sauntered in, sitting next to her mate, Ty.

"We've been waiting for you." He slipped his arm around Tabitha. "Robin, I'm glad you agreed to come here. I believe Adam has shared why we'd like to speak with you."

"Yes. He told me that some book said I might have information to help your search for Pierce. I don't think I'll be able to help you." Robin's shoulders tensed under Adam's fingers.

"I know you've been through hell the last few weeks, and you haven't had much sleep yet, but we have a few questions." Ty leaned forward, his gaze completely on Robin. "Your late husband, Bobby, how did he make contact with Pierce? Was it in person? On the phone?"

"They met during one of Bobby's business trips. I believe when he was in Boston. I'm not sure if that's when they first met. It's definitely where they met the last time. They traveled back and forth from Boston to Virginia occasionally. The police found his…body in Boston." A touch of sorrow tainted her words.

"Where in Boston?" Tabitha leaned forward as if her interest was peaked.

Closing her eyes, Robin ran her hand through her hair. "Copley Square. Why? Do you think that's where Pierce is?"

Ty glanced from Robin to Adam before answering. "It's possible. We've received another lead that has pointed us to Boston. Connor is checking into it."

"Connor, our wolf, is a computer expert," Adam explained, caressing her arm as a shiver ran through her. "How did you know they would come for you?"

"They called me. They let me hear Bobby beg for his life, even offered me to take his place. Bobby's last words, as they tortured him, were for me to run. I gathered a few belongings and ran for my life." True sorrow was now evident in her voice. Tears fell down her cheeks. "I don't know why they killed him, or why he tried to trade my life for his. I honestly don't care. I just want it over. Bobby wasn't the best man and I was debating divorce, but he didn't deserve to be tortured to death."

"For a woman whose husband offered her to a mad man, you seem to have no anger." Tabitha eyed her with suspicious. "I'd be full of hatred."

"I was at first, now…well it doesn't really matter. Bobby is dead. I just want my life back. Can you help me?" Robin asked Tabitha.

"We'll eliminate Pierce and you can do as you wish, until then you need to stay here. Our compound is safe." Ty rose from the sofa, drawing Tabitha with him. "If you don't have any questions, we'll leave you to rest. If you think of anything that might be useful, Adam knows how to reach us."

"How long is this going to take?"

"We've been looking for Pierce for some time. Hopefully Boston will lead us to him. I can't give you an exact time-frame. We want him eliminated as quickly as possible. In the meantime, I hope you'll stay with us. Adam can make other arrangements if you'd like privacy." Ty led Tabitha toward the door where Felix waited.

At the door, Tabitha turned back to Robin. "If you need anything please let us know. Bethany is looking forward to meeting you, and welcoming you to the clan when you're up for visitors. You both went to the same school. She was a few years ahead of you."

"Thanks, Tabitha. Please let Bethany know I'll give her a call when Robin is ready for visitors." Adam stepped around the sofa to sit next to Robin. Sinking down, he wrapped his arm around her shoulders, drawing her close to his body. "I told you there was nothing to worry about. Now why don't you get some rest?"

"Do you think your clan will catch him?" Robin rubbed the leg of her jeans, her body tense under his touch.

With his finger under her chin, he titled her head to look at him. "I know we will. I'm the second to Felix, the Captain of the Guards for Tabitha, which makes me part of the Elder's team. Unlike the other members of the clan, I know what information we have and what we've been doing. I have no doubt we'll take Pierce down. We're closing in on him. It won't be long."

He paused, taking a moment to decide if he wanted to come clean about his own dark past. "I told you before that I was in a situation very similar to yours, where I had to choose to trust someone. More than ten years ago, I was on the run just like you were. There was a rogue who wiped out my family, my parents and two sisters. I wasn't home when it happened. I had gone on a hunting trip with a family friend. When I returned, my home and family were ashes. There was nothing left of what I cherished. I was alone. Without a second thought, I followed the trail, hunting the rogue who killed my parents and my baby sisters. Back then I didn't understand the power of shifting."

The loss of his family still hurt like it was yesterday. He had been close to his sisters with less than two years separating them. The only real division between them was when he went through the change, accepting his beast. They didn't get to reach their change. How he longed to be able to share that part of his life with them. "I chased that rogue from town to town until he turned the chase on me, forcing me to run. I ran, trying to put a plan together because I couldn't leave my family's murder go unpunished. Much like I found you in Texas, Ty found me in a hotel room. He stood by me and we took down the rogue together. We will do it again with Pierce."

"I'm sorry." She laid her hand on his thigh.

"Thank you. It's why I know what you're going through." He wrapped his hand over hers, squeezing it gently. "Things will work out for you as it did for me."

He was certain it wouldn't be long before they found Pierce, which gave Adam a limited amount of time to convince Robin she belonged with him. He'd have to walk a fine line between courting her and respecting her confused emotions.

Chapter Five

In Ty's quarters, Adam leaned against the hard wood chair, exhaustion still seeping from his body. The coffee in his hand helped keep his mind awake. Since arriving back at the compound, sleep had come in spurts between comforting Robin with her fears and nightmares. Performing his duty to the clan by guarding his Queen had taken a backseat for the last few days. He suspected this was why he was called to Ty's.

Ty leaned against the kitchen counter, his hands on either side of him on the granite countertop, his attention on Adam, while his Lieutenant, Raja, sat at the table. No one said anything, but it was a comfortable silence, just as if the Elders were contemplating the situation.

Setting the coffee aside, Adam decided to take control. "I know my duties lie with protecting Tabitha. I apologize for being unable to maintain my role the last few days…"

Ty held up his hand. "That's not the reason we've called you here today. But since you brought up your position, you will have to find a balance between Robin and your duty to the clan, if you wish to remain part of Tabitha's guards."

"Yes sir. My devotion to the clan and to guarding Tabitha hasn't changed." Adam glanced from Ty to Raja before turning his attention back to Ty. "Robin has been having extreme panic attacks. I've been trying to help. Once Bethany visits with Robin, she might be able to help. A woman might be able to offer more comfort. She also understands what Robin is going through. The only comfort I can give her is my touch, and while it helps, it's not a permanent solution."

"I'll bring Bethany over this evening." Raja sat his coffee mug on the counter.

Adam questioned the absence of the women. "Where are Tabitha and Bethany? Is there a new threat to their safety?"

"Nothing new." Ty shook his head. "Tabitha and Bethany were meeting with Kallie to consult the new tigress, Harmony, who stumbled upon our clan injured while you were away. She's young, maybe twenty, and has been on her own for a while. She's been in hiding, living in the woods, mostly in her tigress form. She stepped onto a bear trap. The wound on her leg is pretty rough, and being malnourished is making her health worse. She's not healing like she should."

"Is her story the truth?" Adam was concerned this new tigress could be an enemy, sent to gain their trust. As one of the Elders guards, he had to be aware of everyone as a potential threat to their safety, especially with Pierce still on the loose.

"She refuses to speak. She's scared and won't shift from her tigress form. Tabitha is going to try to speak with her using her ability to communicate by thought, as she did with Lukas when he arrived injured at her welcome home party." Ty ran his hand through his shoulder length hair, drawing it away from his face.

"Besides Felix, are other guards with the women? Why did she need Bethany and Kallie? If the young tigress strikes out in fear, one of the women could be injured." Adam mentally kicked himself for not performing his duties. He should be with Tabitha, to protect her from the new tigress, not sitting here with the Elders, or cuddling Robin as he had earlier.

"Felix is with her and Thomas is filling in for you temporarily. Shadow, Styx, and the twins, Drew and Jayden, of Bethany's guards are also with them. They're protected. I believe either Taber or Thorben accompanied

Kallie, as they rarely let her go anywhere without one of them." Ty stepped closer to the table, pulling out a chair and sitting down. "Robin is holding back. Whatever she's hiding is causing these panic attacks, and it's more than being frightened by shifters. She trusts you. You're the only one close enough to find out what she's hiding without us adding pressure."

"I'll do whatever you need, but Robin's trust for me is flimsy. She is only with me because she has no one else. Give her someone else that she believes is more trustworthy, or isn't a shifter and she'll cling to them." Adam hated that his words were the truth. Robin was his mate and he wanted to gain her trust, but she was like a scared child hiding in a corner, not really trusting anyone.

"You're her mate. You'll find a way to completely gain her trust, as I did with Bethany." Raja gave him an encouraging smile.

Adam nodded, not completely convinced. "Has Connor found anything in Boston yet?"

Ty shook his head, disappointment clear on his face. "He's eliminating leads. Jinx's clan is standing by in West Virginia if we find a solid lead they can follow."

"Do you trust his team?" Adam had begun to accept Jinx as a part of their team, but since he hadn't met any of the West Virginia Tigers other than Jinx and Lukas, Adam wasn't sure if they were trustworthy. Before Lukas took a position with Connor, dealing with the technical aspect of the search for Pierce, he had been Jinx's unofficial second, helping him command the West Virginia Tigers.

"We've already sent two of our men for additional support there, but I trust Jinx's clan." Ty leaned forward, placing his hands on the table. "If we have solid evidence Pierce is in Boston some of us will go. Hopefully, we'll have time to get there before he moves on. I want to be there when he goes down."

Adam swallowed the last drink of his coffee, and pushed back his chair. He wanted to ask his Alpha if he could be a part of the take-down team, but now wasn't the time. It would be putting the cart before the horse. He'd wait for the right time to approach that subject. "Once I find out if she's hiding any information, I'll let you know."

Ty nodded. "We don't have a lot of time. We need to find Pierce before he attacks again, and before he finds out Robin is here. The compound doesn't need another attack."

"I'll try to be quick." He turned his attention to Raja. "I'll see you and Bethany tonight."

Leaving Ty's quarters, he followed Tabitha's scent. Even knowing there were other guards with her, he needed to check on her. Since Tabitha's arrival in Alaska, Felix and Adam had developed a bond that made them a strong team. They predicted each other's move, giving them the best advantage to protect the Queen of the Tigers. No matter how well trained the other guards were, they just weren't Adam. He wouldn't risk Tabitha's safety. She was too important to not only the clan, but to all tigers, and shifters.

There had to be a balance between his duties to the Queen, and his obligation to Robin. Other guards established the balance, so why wouldn't he? Sitting in front of his Elders, Adam should have been concerned with his responsibilities to his clan, instead he couldn't stop thinking about Robin. He longed for her touch, to get her to fully trust him.

Now that he was mated, he understood why so many of the guards, who went through the mating, were temporarily given leave from their duties. A guard couldn't perform their job to the fullest if their head was always thinking about their mate. When guarding the clan, especially the Elders, a guard had to commit to them completely. It was only natural to be worried about a mate, but a guard couldn't hinder their ability to protect the clan.

Ultimately, protecting the clan as a whole would protect a mate.

Adam walked around the building to where most of the unmated clan members lived. Thomas leaned causally next to one of the doors. Adam worked with Thomas long enough to know that even if he appeared to be relaxed and at ease, he'd spring to action faster than many of the other guards. Drew and Jayden stood with their legs spread apart and arms crossed. They were alert as if expecting danger at any moment. They appeared more like bodyguards, but they were young and new to guarding the Elders.

"Hey, Adam, what are you doing here? Ty said you were taking a few days off." Thomas stood straight.

"I had some stuff to deal with, but wanted to check on Felix and Tabitha." Adam didn't have the same easiness with Thomas as he did with Felix, but they were still partners from time to time. He didn't want to explain his situation with Robin to Thomas. If Ty wanted Thomas to know Robin was here then he would have told the guard.

"They're inside," Drew said, as if Felix and Tabitha's whereabouts weren't obvious.

Adam nodded and moved pass them to the door. Stepping inside, he heard a growl erupt from the tigress lying next to the bed. He went into protection mode, reaching for the firearm strapped to his hip.

"Don't shoot. She's just terrified." Tabitha turned to face Adam, doing the one thing you never did when a dangerous predator eyed you like dinner, she turned her back on the animal.

Felix automatically stepped between the Queen and the tigress, blocking the tigress if she decided to attack.

"Tabitha, what the hell are you thinking?" Adam wanted to rush to his charge, but he didn't want to spook the tigress any more than she already was. He placed his hands on Tabitha's arms and spun her around to the tigress. "You know better than to turn your back on a possible threat."

Nodding, she glanced across at Adam. "I wasn't thinking."

"Even with guards around you, you can't take risks like that. It's dangerous." He was glad this situation didn't get out of control because of her mistake. She meant too much to the future of shifters for her to be careless.

"What are you doing here?"

"My job." Adam needed to make sure something like this didn't happen again. He looked around the small studio. Bethany and Kallie stood off to the side, Shadow and Styx protecting Bethany, as Adam should have been doing for Tabitha with Felix. Thorben stood next to his mate, Kallie. Thorben and Taber were part of the Kodiak Bears out of Nome before mating with Kallie and becoming honorary Alaskan Tigers. "Have you gained anything more from this tigress?"

"Very little. Her fears have taken over her thoughts. I know she can hear me in her head because she responds to me with her eyes, but I think the connection frightens her even more." Tabitha kept her attention on the tigress, her shoulders rigid as if heeding Adam's warning to never let down her guard.

"Did you get any negative readings from her?"

"No, Harmony is just scared. I've gathered she's been on her own most of her life." Tabitha tried to take a step closer to the tigress, only to be stopped by Felix.

"You're close enough," Felix told her without removing his stare from the tigress.

"Guards always make my job harder." She knelt, going eye level with Harmony, also making the duty of protecting her more difficult for the guards if something happened. Unnerving, but part of their job, they couldn't keep Tabitha sheltered so much it hindered her duties to the clan and the rest of the tigers.

"Harmony, I know you're scared, but you're safe here. No one is going to hurt you. We need to know where you were injured, if it was truly a hunter's trap or one set up for our kind. If we're going to protect you, we need to know if someone is after you." After a few minutes of silence, Tabitha finally stood. "It's no use, there are too many people. All of the men here are scaring her even more. If I'm going to get anything from her then you guys need to leave."

"Not happening Tabitha, you know the rules," Ty said from the back of the room, causing everyone to turn.

Adam had been so immersed in what was happening he wasn't paying attention to the door as a bodyguard should, even though the guards outside would have kept anyone out that meant harm. Drew and Jayden were young, and eager to prove themselves.

Harmony growled. Tigers rarely retreat when frightened. Being predators, they'd fight to the death. Harmony would run if there were an opening. The studio apartment they had put her in left very little room for her in tigress form. She could only cower or fight. Right now she chose to cower, but that could change in an instant.

"Harmony, it's okay. Ty's the Alpha here and my mate. He means you no harm. Actually Ty and Raja, our Lieutenant, are the ones who found you stumbling around the woods." Tabitha beckoned her mate to stand next to her. Snuggling into his body, she glanced up at him. "This isn't working, Ty."

"Compromise," Ty whispered, loud enough that Adam heard. "Kallie, Tabitha thought having an additional female, that wasn't an Elder, would help, but it's not working. If you and Thorben could leave."

"Tabitha, if you need me, you know where I am. Good luck." Kallie quietly made an exit with Thorben at her side.

Adam waited beside Tabitha, waiting for Ty to dismiss him. He wanted to stay, to do his duty, but he also knew Ty expected him to get to the bottom of whatever Robin was hiding.

Instead of dismissing him, Ty turned to Styx. "If you could wait outside with the others."

As Adam was Felix's right hand, Styx was Shadow's. They rarely separated when protecting Bethany. They too where a well-tuned pair, knowing each other's moves.

With Styx's exit, Ty focused on Tabitha. "That's the best you get. Without Raja here, I trust the four of us to keep you and Bethany safe. Do what you need because time's running short."

"Maybe I should try healing her." Bethany suggested. "If she's not in so much pain maybe she won't be so scared."

Ty shook his head. "Not happening until she's calmer. Doc gave her something for the pain, but until she's calm enough that we can get close without the risk of her attacking, we won't jeopardize you or Galen."

Tabitha closed her eyes as she tried to reason with the scared tigress. "Harmony, if you could relax, Bethany can try to heal your leg." Suddenly her eyes opened, her body rigidly tense. "Felix, go outside now."

"What?" Felix frowned.

"Go outside. Send in Styx, anyone, just go." There was desperation in her voice that Adam had never heard before.

"Just go, Felix," Ty ordered. The authority in his voice made it clear that Tabitha wouldn't have asked if there wasn't a reason behind it.

Felix shrugged his shoulders and left without another word. Adam stepped into Felix's vacated spot, ready to jump in front of Tabitha, to protect her if the situation called for it.

"He's not the man you fear, I swear it. Felix is the Captain of my Guards and has been a member of this clan since he came into his tiger." Tabitha words were meant to reassure the tigress.

Hopefully Tabitha's plan would work with the tigress because Adam was confused. He didn't understand why Harmony would fear Felix. He wasn't small by any means, but he was less intimidating then their Alpha. Ty had an air of authority no one else matched, not even Jinx, the West Virginia Alpha.

Chapter Six

More than an hour later, Adam was in the conference room with the Elders and their guards. He was anxious to get back to Robin, but the questions running through his head could only be answered by Tabitha, who left him waiting with everyone else.

Ty's arm sat tight around Tabitha's waist. He glanced around the room as everyone gathered. "Recent information has come to light that everyone here needs to know." He turned to Felix and held his hand up for the guard to stand. "Felix, please share this information with us."

Pushing away from the table, Felix rose from his chair. "The clan members who were around when I was a child might remember my story, but it is never spoken about. It's not something the Elders or I publicized. We preferred to keep my personal issues private." He paused, gazing out the window as if unable to meet anyone's gaze. "I have a twin brother, Henry. Since the clan moved to Alaska, he's been living with a clan in Ohio. To my knowledge, Henry is the first child of two shifter parents who can't shift. The tiger inside him wants to shift, but his body won't let him. Being unable to shift is driving him insane."

Felix's hands clenched into balls. "We both had the same symptoms—fever, body aches, pains, and stomach cramps. When the time came to shift, I shifted. My brother said he could feel the tiger clawing at the inside of his body, but the change wouldn't happen. We took him to Doc. He couldn't determine the reason. Henry went through a number of treatments to bring the tiger out. All options available were explored. Nothing worked. The agony became too much for him. The vibrant twin I grew up with is no longer there. He is, for all purposes, insane. He fights anyone who gets close, so he has to be heavily drugged. Even though he's not in tiger form, he's still deadly. Henry has the strength and speed of a tiger. The Ohio Tigers have a doctor who works with mentally ill patients. He has been looking after my brother for some time. Henry is allowed to live among the clan as long as he is treated by their doctor." Felix spit out the truth about his family and then turned to face everyone in the silent room.

"Doc is great, he just doesn't have the experience with the mentally ill to help Henry. I visit my brother as much as I can. Most times, he doesn't know who I am, regardless of his condition, I continued to visit him. When Ty found Tabitha in Pennsylvania, I was in Ohio visiting Henry. When Ty asked for help guarding her, I left Henry and rushed to their side. My last visit to Ohio was the last time I saw Henry. I had no idea…" He shook his head.

Adam didn't need to feel Felix's emotions to know the man was tormented by his brother's metal health. Felix had no mate to ease his torment, so he had to endure the pain alone. "You had no idea of what?" Adam encouraged him to carry on with his story.

"Anyone who didn't live up to the clan's standards, who was considered lesser tigers, was sent to my brother's quarters where he tortured them." Felix ran his hand over his face, before meeting Adam's gaze. "It kept him calm and quiet. You have to know, I wouldn't have agreed if I had known."

"If you didn't know, then how do we know now?" Styx asked.

"I learned it from Harmony. Once we cleared the room of some of the guards, I was able to connect telepathically with her. I saw the memories. It was clear why she was running. She thought Henry and Felix were the same person. It's why I sent him from the room," Tabitha explained.

Adam processed the information quickly, putting together the pieces. He knew Felix had a brother that he visited, but the rest was all new to Adam.

"If Harmony was considered lesser to them, why wasn't Henry?"

Tabitha shot Felix a look before answering. "All I've been able to gather is Henry proved to be helpful to the clan. I suspect by killing those they believed didn't belong, Henry held a usefulness for them, as well as income from what Felix was paying them to care for his twin."

Adam tried to wrap his head around Felix's horrifying description of events. "We know all of this because Harmony was one of the tigers given to Henry?"

"Yes." Felix's one word response caused a whispered hush over the room.

Robin tried to read, but no book had any appeal to her. She pushed the curtain aside and peeked out window. More tigers covered the grounds. There was no way she could sneak away from the compound if there was never a break in the guards. Staying here wasn't an option. She had second thoughts about the whole situation. They wouldn't want her here once they found out she knew more than she shared. She had to find a way to escape, not that she had a plan, or even a winter jacket suitable for Alaska. April in Alaska was quite chilly. Robin wouldn't survive long without shelter.

Stepping to the side of the window, out of the direct view of anyone who might be looking, she caught a glimpse of her reflection in the window. Dark circles shadowed her eyes like an awful makeup job. All of the color, that normally tinted her cheeks, was gone, leaving her pale. Her long, curly brown hair fell lifeless over her shoulders, her highlights having outgrown weeks ago. Running for her life had left little time to go to the salon for a touch-up. The girl next-door look she always resembled was gone, and replaced with something the cat dragged in. *I guess the cat did drag it in.* She chuckled at her twisted sense of humor.

Running from state to state, she had two goals, to stay alive and to live again. Yet here she was, in a compound of shifters she was running from. She may never have another chance at a normal life. Not like she had before. She couldn't get her job back, what would she tell her boss? If she told him a bunch of shapeshifters were after her, her boss would call the paddy wagon. This meant if she managed to escape with her life, she'd never be able to return to Virginia without questions being raised. No one in her small town would give her a job after she disappeared from the last one without notice.

What was the point of running when nothing was left of the life she cherished? Maybe giving up the fight now and letting things play out how they were meant to, was the best option, even if it meant her life. The front door opened, bursting her thoughts. She stepped into the shadow of the curtains, hiding from whoever entered. Staying undercover helped keep her alive up to this point.

"Robin, it's only me." Adam glanced around the cabin, his sense of smell quickly narrowing in on her. He shut the door and walked toward her, his hands in the air, still trying to reassure her that he meant no harm.

Moving away from the curtain, she pushed away the thoughts of running. She didn't want Adam to get suspicious. "Do your friends want me to leave?"

"You're not the reason I met with the Elders. I have commitments to the clan, to keep the Alpha's mate safe. They needed to know when I would be able to step back into my position. As the second of Tabitha's guards, my unavailability is straining on the Captain of her Guards, Felix." Adam leaned against the arm of the chair and sighed.

"I don't mean to hold you back from your duties. If you could give me a ride to an airport or car rental company, I'll get out of your hair." She was successful at keeping the anticipation from her voice, but she doubted it went missing from her scent. She wasn't used to anyone being able to smell her emotions.

Shaking his head, he smiled at her. "You're trying hard, but you can't hide anything from your mate. You're not getting away that easy." He approached her, reaching out to place his hands on her arms. "I know you're scared. I swear I'll protect you. I need to know what you're so scared of. What are you hiding? Please, tell me and I'll help you."

"The only thing to say is, I shouldn't be here. I need to go. They're going to find me. I'm a risk for your clan, and your Elders. Just take me to the airport." It was stupid to hold out for hope that he'd let her walk out of his life. She didn't want to deal with any of this. Was having a normal life too much to ask for?

"That's not going to happen. Even if rogues weren't after you, I wouldn't let you walk away from our connection."

"There's nothing between us. Nothing." She stressed her words, hoping he'd take the hint. He seemed like a nice guy, and her body was affected by him, but she didn't want to get involved with the same kind she was running from. Robin couldn't befriend a shifter no matter how much they tried to probe into her life.

"There will be, you'll see. We're meant to be together. First, I have to gain your trust." He slid his hands up and down her arms. "As your mate, I *can't* lie to you, and you could feel a lie if you focused."

"What do you mean?" Fear ran through her mind. It was one thing for him to feel her emotions, but to know she was lying…how would she keep anything from him? She had to get out of here.

"Come sit and I'll show you." He slipped his hand into hers, leading her toward the sofa. Once they were both sitting, he turned to face her. "Clear your mind and focus. Ready?"

She nodded, unsure what to expect. She was as relaxed and focused as possible under the circumstances.

"I'm a guard for the Queen of the Tigers." He paused, as if letting his statement sink in. "Do you feel the truth to the statement—the sweetness on the back of your tongue, the honesty in the words?"

Running her tongue over the top of her mouth, she took in the taste. "I don't know. I mean, I guess. I do have a sweet taste in my mouth, almost like rich chocolate."

"Now, feel the difference with this one." He gave her a moment to focus again. "I work for Pierce and he sent me to find you."

Her body stiffened and a lump formed in her throat. When he laid his hand over hers, she fought the urge to pull away.

"I know that statement frightens you. It's only a test for you to be able to sense the lie. Focus on my words. The hairs on the back of your neck should be standing, the air should be heavy and harder to breathe, and the taste in your mouth changed. It's now coppery. Those are the signs that it's a lie. Can you feel them?"

Her mind screamed for her to run. Surprisingly, everything he described was there. "How can that be?"

"It's a safety feature for mates. If we were in a situation where a lie might be needed, our mate would know we were lying. Shifter mates have a couple of safety features, that's one of them. The connection will get stronger once the mating is complete. Other links will develop as well. Since you're not a shifter, you don't understand the full process. Your body isn't recognizing the signs yet, but you will. I can feel your emotions without even thinking about it. It's why I know you're hiding something. Tell me, so I can help."

Sidestepping his last comment, she changed the subject back to the bond shifters have. "What abilities do the other shifters have?"

"Some shifters can communicate through thoughts, especially in stressful situations. Some can only do it when in their animal form. Tabitha is able to communicate in human form with animals, and in both forms with her mate. It's rare but as she's our Queen, she'll have abilities others don't." He ran this thumb over Robin's knuckles. "You're avoiding my question. What are you hiding?"

"Please, Adam, I can't." She couldn't tell him, fearing it would jeopardize her safety. His clan would no longer protect her or they'd want her killed for the same reason Pierce did. If only she had never told Bobby, then no one would know. Why did she think she could trust Bobby? He'd sell his best friend's soul to the devil if it got him out of whatever trouble he was in.

"Robin, you're going to have to trust me if you want me to keep you safe. I can't help you if I don't know what I'm supposed to protect you from."

She shot up from the sofa, putting distance between them. "Damn it, I don't need you to watch over me. I was doing fine before. Just let me leave and you won't have to worry about me."

"Running from state to state, and from motel to motel, you call that doing fine? That's no life. You can't run like a scared animal for the rest of your life. We need to stand together and remove what you're running from. Robin, you're not the only one running from Pierce's gang of rogues. He's killed people I care about. He's got a long list of deaths in his wake. I don't want to see your name on that list." He pushed from the sofa. She could sense the anger rolling off him in thick waves. He stood in front of her. "Why won't you trust me? Do you not understand what kind of danger you're in? You have to help me, help you. That's the only way we're going to work."

"It's not that I don't want your help. I just don't know how to accept it. I don't want to live like I have been. To trust you and your clan is asking a lot from me. What happens when you find out my secret? You'll want nothing to do with me. Then I've risked everything and I'm back to square one." Tears welled in her eyes, threatening to fall. She tried to hold them back. Her hesitation boiled down to not wanting to be alone, and not wanting to run anymore. She longed to be able to trust Adam, to have him by her side, even after he discovered her secret.

He reached out to her. She wanted to accept his touch yet she refused herself the luxury. Any contact with Adam right now would be the final straw that broke the dam holding back her tears. Taking a step aside, she watched him frown and his hand fell away. She saw the disappointment clear in his eyes.

"Like it or not, I'm your mate. Even though we haven't completed the mating, we are still bound. It's my job to keep you safe. I'll protect you. You're not getting rid of me, no matter how hard you try. I swear you won't be alone again. Please let me help you."

In that instant, she almost told him everything. It would be such a relief to confide in someone. Before she could come clean, his cell phone rang, stealing the moment and once again returning those second thoughts to the forefront.

Chapter Seven

Adam clipped his cell phone on his belt, watching Robin from the kitchen. If Ty hadn't called, she would have told him what she was hiding. The delay wouldn't stop him from getting to the truth. He swallowed a mouthful of water, and then tossed the bottle in the trash before walking into the living room to confront her again.

"Everything okay?" She turned away from the window to face him.

"Who is Eugene German?"

Her face paled more than he thought possible. He was concerned she was going to faint. Her anxiety coursed through him as if it was his own. He wanted to go to her, to tell her that whatever she was hiding she didn't have to tell him, but he couldn't offer her that comfort. The clan's need for this information weighed more than a little discomfort for his mate. Adam couldn't risk more innocent people dying because his mate didn't understand the evil they were up against.

"Robin, why does that name instill fear in you? You need to tell me who he is. We don't have time to play games here. Pierce will kill again. Are you willing to risk someone's life because of this secret?" He had to get this information before Raja and Bethany stopped by this evening. Raja would definitely not have as much patience, and Adam didn't want to put his mate through a grueling interrogation.

"He's dead," she blurted out.

"I know that. What I need to know is who he is. What is your connection to him?"

She stepped toward the sofa, sinking onto it, no longer met his gaze. "He was my father. He died a year ago. What does he have to do with this?"

"Connor found information on him. I want to hear it from you." He sat beside her, taking her hand in his. He hoped to give her what comfort he could. "Tell me."

"My father was a scientist. A few months before he died, one of his office assistants came to him, begging for help. She was bit by a shifter and wanted to know if there was a way to reverse the effects. I don't have any proof. I believe it was Pierce or one of his main people. Bobby said some things about Pierce that led me to believe this. My father wasn't able to find an immediate cure and didn't have time to complete his studies, because his car was run off the road. He died at the crash site. I can't make heads or tails of his notes, but I think Pierce believed my father was close to a discovery that might have cured anyone bitten. He had my father killed." Tears fell down her cheeks.

"How do you know someone connected to Pierce killed your father?"

"It wasn't a connection, it *was* Pierce. Damn it! He made Bobby drive the car that ran my father off the road, and I was on the phone when it happened. It was just like the night Pierce killed Bobby. Pierce always wanted me to know, every damn time he had me on the phone." Talking about Bobby reminded her of the night he was murdered. "Our marriage was over long before that night, but to hear Bobby trade my life for his confirmed the end. The night before Pierce killed Bobby, I reviewed my father's notes from the tests he ran on his assistant. Bobby told Pierce what I read, making Pierce's desire to find me even stronger."

Adam removed his hand from hers and pulled her against him. "I'll protect you, I promise."

"You said I don't know what Pierce is capable of. I do, he killed two people I cared about. I don't want to be another notch on his belt." Leaning into his embrace, she rested her head on his chest.

"We're closing in on him. We just have to find his location." His hand slid down her arm.

"He's mainly in Boston. He also has a place in Virginia where he goes often. Bobby met Pierce on one of his trips to Boston. His company had a branch in Boston and he did a lot of work out of Virginia as well."

He lifted her chin with his finger, titling her head so he could gaze into her eyes. "Do you know the address?"

Nodding, her eyes reflected fear again. "I have Bobby's calendar. He kept notes on everything. But you can't go. Pierce will kill you." Her fingers dug into his shirt, balling it into fists and scratching his skin. "Please, I don't want to be alone again. Don't go!"

"Shhh, love. Nothing's going to happen to me." He hugged her tight. "I need his calendar, and your father's notes. Doc might be able to decipher them."

An hour later, Adam stood next to Robin in the conference room. Her fear nearly made the air unbreathable. Being surrounded by the Elders and their guards was more than she could handle, so thankfully the Elders understood she wouldn't be able to tell them what they needed to know if fear controlled her. With that in mind, only Ty, Tabitha, Raja, Bethany, and Felix were present in the room.

"Robin, Doc is going through your father's notes now, and Connor is searching the addresses in Bobby's book. Did Bobby ever mention anything particular about any of the places? Maybe Pierce's favorite stops on his travels, something that might narrow the search down?" Ty sat next to his mate, watching Robin. To Ty's credit he tried to sound less intimidating, but as the Alpha, it was nearly impossible for him to sound less authoritative than what he was.

Adam sensed ripples of fear running through Robin. Even with his arms around her it wasn't enough to get her past the panic that hung in the balance He kissed her temple and nuzzled his body against hers. "It's okay, Love."

"Adam's right, there's nothing to fear. We mean you no harm, Robin. Our goal is to take Pierce and his gang of rogues down. His demise will keep you, our mates, and our clan safe. Once we learn more, you and Adam can go back to his cabin. We'll do our best to give you the time you need to adjust to your mate, and this whole situation." Ty leaned forward, placing his hand on the table. Tabitha then laid her hand over his.

Robin shook her head. "I don't want to see anyone else get hurt. If I tell you where Pierce might be, someone else could be killed."

"Shapeshifters are a little more resistant than weres that were bitten like Pierce," Tabitha said. "I don't want anyone to get hurt, especially from my clan, but if we don't stop him he *will* kill again. We have to remove Pierce and his gang before more innocent people die."

"We'd rather take the fight to him, than risk our women and children," Ty added. "Connor and Lukas are very good at what they do. They'll narrow the search even without you. However the time you could save us, might prevent another death."

Adam understood his Alpha's persistence. Robin's delay could cost a life. Shifters had benefits over bitten weres. Humans had nothing. They were easy prey. Pierce had already proven he had no quarrels about killing anyone in his way. "Love, we need to know more about Pierce's location in order to keep you and our clan safe. The longer the delay, the higher the risk is for all of us. We left Pierce's men back in Texas, but it won't take long before they realize I brought you to Alaska. Pierce will come up with a plan, sending the rogues here after you and the clan. That will give us some time. I'd rather take him down before he can devise a plan of attack on the compound."

Adam wasn't completely sure Pierce wouldn't risk his men without a plan. Adam kept that thought to himself to keep Robin from being more on edge. He'd protect his mate from the evil of Pierce and the dangers of shifter life as long as he could. She was fragile, never having any experience with shifters until Pierce dragged her into it. Robin had spirit, but everything she had gone through the last few months had taken its toll. She was probably inches away from a complete breakdown. Shifter life wasn't for the weak. If Robin gained enough confidence, it would make her a stronger woman and a stronger mate.

She let out a deep sigh, and nodded. "I accompanied Bobby to Boston on a business trip, to visit a friend who lived there. The address in Boston is for a warehouse. I had to wait outside for him, so I can't give you the layout. It's on the outskirts of town and there's nothing around. They knew we were coming before we arrived because they called Bobby's cell to tell me I had to wait in the car at the gate while he went in. The gate was maybe a hundred and fifty feet from the building. They'll see you first. It will be a death trap. Please, there's got to be another way."

"I didn't say we would attack there, we just need to know about the location. We'll figure out something that will swing the favor in our direction. I won't risk my people unless I believe we can kill Pierce." Ty turned in his chair. "Felix, get Connor on the phone."

While Felix called Connor on the conference room phone, Raja stepped away from Bethany's chair. "Was there a set schedule when Pierce would be in Boston over the place in Virginia?"

"Bobby's travels were the same sometimes. Maybe if you look in his calendar. We didn't talk about Pierce often. I didn't even know about him until Bobby got in trouble and went to Pierce to bail him out." Robin's body stiffened under Adam's hands. "There's a house in Virginia. I believe Bobby said he was there a lot, always alone. That area might be your best course of action if you're going to attack before Pierce does. It might give you an advantage you won't have in Boston, but I don't know if he's there."

"Don't worry, we have scouts to find him and then we'll get a plan in place," Ty said, as Felix scooted the phone across the table to him. "Connor, you there?"

"I'm here. I was going through Bobby's calendar. I think I found a pattern." The wolf shifter's voice was rattled from the background noise of computers. Connor's fingers could be heard speeding across the keyboard. Their geek wolf shifter was always busy on his computer unless he was asleep.

"Good. See if you can figure out if Pierce is in Virginia. If not, then where he might be." Ty turned to Tabitha when she placed her hand on his.

"Connor, the address in Virginia is Victor's house. Find out everything you can about it. There was work done. It has a hidden room, and I think there's someone living in it." Tabitha frowned.

"Someone is hiding out in that room?" The sound of Connor's fingers typing on the keyboard stopped, leaving an eerie silence over the phone.

"I saw it in Victor's thoughts. It didn't make sense then. Hurry, Connor, I can't explain why, but I know urgency is a must." Tabitha squeezed her eyes shut.

"I will. I'll get Lukas in here to look into Boston so I can focus on the house in Virginia. I'll contact you as soon as I find anything." Connor ended the call.

"Tabby, what is it?" Ty wrapped his arm around the back of his mate.

"I can't put my finger on it. I just know we have to hurry. I need time to put all the pieces together. Everything I saw in Victor's head is a jumbled mess in my head now." She leaned her head against Ty's shoulder.

"I'm going to take Tabitha back to our quarters." Ty rose, holding

Tabitha's hand. "Robin, if you think of anything, please let us know. Adam, meet me in my quarters eight tonight. If Connor finds information before then, we'll contact you." Ty and Tabitha left the room, Felix falling into step behind them.

Bethany rose from her chair and walked to Robin and Adam. "I'm not sure if you remember me or not. I'm Bethany Thompson, now Bethany Harrison. I was a few years ahead of you in school. I knew Bobby. I'm sorry for your loss and for everything you're dealing with. I know you're scared to be here, surrounded by so many shifters, but it is the safest place for you."

"I remember seeing you around school. How did you end up here? Are you...?"

"No, I'm not a shifter. Raja rescued me from the clutches of one of Pierce's men. I'm mated to Raja and this is my home now." Bethany slid her arm around Raja's waist, avoiding the gun sitting in his shoulder holster.

"What about your family? Surely they don't approve of you being with a shifter. Or aren't they allowed to know about his second nature?" The astonishment was clear in Robin's voice.

"Pierce killed my parents and my younger sister, Jamie. If they were alive, they would want me happy, and Raja makes me happy. Being a shifter isn't something to be ashamed of, or for others to think less of them. I'm proud to have a shifter mate. He stands up for those who can't. It doesn't matter if they are shifters or human, Raja and the rest of the Alaskan Tigers will fight for them. I couldn't have asked for a better man to have by my side." Bethany smiled at her mate. The love they shared was clear.

Adam had told her that Bethany's family was one of Pierce's victims, her words had been heartless. If Robin could get Bethany to see through whatever spell it was that Raja had on her, maybe it wasn't too late to save her. "What about your future? You're willing to give up children? A normal life? Everything?"

With Robin's questions, Adam's body tensed. He quickly realized she wasn't accepting their mating as he had hoped. She might only be accepting his touch because of the comfort it brought her, not because she was acknowledging their mating. "You don't have to give up anything just because you're mated to a shifter," Adam explained. "You can still have children. With only one shifter parent, they'd have a fifty-fifty shot of being a shifter. Being mated to a shifter doesn't mean you can't have a normal life, or even better than what you consider normal."

Robin turned to face Adam, anger coloring her green eyes. "Normal? How can you consider your world anywhere near normal? Normal isn't living in a compound with fences and barbwire around the top, guards on patrol at all times, and you sure as hell don't have meetings to discuss murdering someone."

"The barbwire and guards are not to keep us in, but to keep people out who would like to see us dead. There are humans who have discovered our kind and they would rather see us dead than to breathe the same air they do. As for murdering Pierce, that is no different than what your government would do. Would you prefer we let him live? How much longer do you think you could have survived if I didn't find you in Texas?" Adam's own anger rose to match hers.

"The clan is allowed to leave as they see fit." Raja explained. "Most prefer to stay on our land for the safety, but there are others who travel outside our gates daily. We're not so different from humans. We just choose to live in the safety of the compound. We're not here because we're a danger to you or anyone else." Raja glanced at Bethany. "Come love, Tora is expecting us." He led Bethany to the door before turning back to Adam. "Good luck." Raja winked.

When the door closed, and they were alone in the room, Robin stepped away from Adam. "What the hell was that supposed to mean?"

Robin obviously took offense to Raja's last comment. Adam thought it best not to get into that conversation, knowing it would only irritate her further. Instead, he moved to the door. "We should get back to my cabin. I have work I need to attend do." He walked to the door, hoping she'd follow. He wanted to pack a bag just in case word came back that he was one of the men going to Virginia or Boston to take down Pierce. To guarantee he was on the list, he whipped out his cell and sent Ty a quick text message. He didn't want to mention it to Robin. Her fears were already escalated.

Chapter Eight

Robin stood in the doorway of Adam's bedroom, completely shocked he was stuffing a duffle bag with clothes. "Where are you going?"

He opened the bedside table and pulled out magazine cartridges for his gun. "I'm heading the team that goes after Pierce. Once his location is confirmed, my orders are to fly out with some of the guards. I need to be ready."

"You're what?" She shook her head. "What about me?"

Placing his weapons on top of his clothes, he turned to her. "You're going to stay with Bethany while I'm gone. You'll be safe with her and her guards, but no more comments about how shifters don't live up to your standards, or that we are less because we have two forms."

"No. I want to be taken to the airport."

"Damn it, Robin, I'm trying to protect you. Bethany and Tabitha will have double the guards on them until we've taken down Pierce. You'll be safe with them, safer than on your own. I don't want to hear anymore about it. If you want to leave when this is over, fine. It's not happening until then."

She crossed her arms over her chest, feeling like a child being scolded. "I just want this to be over."

He stepped to her, close enough to touch. "That's what we're trying to do."

"Why does it have to be you?"

"It's my job. With Ty going, I need to be there to watch his back, and Felix needs to stay behind to protect Tabitha. Ty is my Alpha, not to mention my Queen's mate. She needs him to carry on our line. Without them, all tigers will cease to exist. I won't let Ty go alone. I'm sorry, I just can't. Please try to understand, these people gave me a home and the opportunity to prove myself as a guard. I won't let them down, not when I'm needed the most." Pulling off his shirt, he stepped away from her. "I'm going for a run."

Robin stayed where she was as he stripped down and walked out the front door. A large Bengal tiger then ran past the windows. She sank to the floor, cradling her head in her hands and cried. Honestly, she had nothing against shifters, at least not the Alaskan Tigers and especially not Adam. She used her fight as an excuse to avoid getting close to him. She was tired of being hurt and of being abandoned. If Adam went after Pierce he might not come back. She couldn't run the risk of attaching to him. Everyone she cared about was being picked off one-by-one by Pierce and his gang, leaving her alone and scared. She wasn't sure she had the will to stay alive if Adam wasn't by her side. *Damn him, for making me care about him.*

Adam ran until his lungs begged for oxygen and his paws cried from exhaustion. It still didn't clear his mind or remove the need to claim Robin. If anything, being in his tiger form added to the mating desire. He wanted Robin with every ounce of his body.

Sneaking in the backdoor, by the master bedroom, he hoped to avoid her. Seeing her while being naked from a run would do little to keep his remaining control in check, especially with his beast so close to the surface. He, like most shifters, had very little problem with being naked, but nudity led to only one thing when the mating desire was fully upon a shifter. He stepped into the master bathroom without considering the possibility Robin could have been there.

"Ahhh!" She slid under the water, covering herself with bubbles before surfacing. "I'm sorry. You were gone so long and the garden tub called to me. I thought it would be okay."

"It's fine. I'll shower in the guest bath." He longed for the mating to be complete—to slip in the tub next to her.

"Wait. I'm sorry about before. I'm just tired of seeing everyone I care for die. I don't want you to be next. Will you reconsider?"

He tried to stop staring, because in that moment to claim her body, he would have sold his soul. The mating desire rode him hard, leaving his body aching for her touch. "For you, I'd do almost anything, but not this. I'll be back, I promise."

"You can't keep a promise like that. I'll sit around here waiting for you to come back with no way of knowing if you're okay or not."

He couldn't keep his gaze adverted any longer. Her head rested against the back of the tub, her long brown hair lay in wet strands surrounding her shoulders, the curls were gone from the weight of the water, and tears streamed down her cheeks. "There is a way for you to know." He shook his head. No, he wouldn't use the benefits of mating to claim her before she was ready. "Never mind. I need to shower."

She sat up straight, bubbles cascaded down her body, making him want to lick each drop. "Tell me."

"Mating allows you to feel your mate, to know what they are going through even when miles separate you. If our mating was consummated, you would be able to sense me, to know if I was okay or uninjured. It would also make it impossible for you to leave at the end, if you choose this life isn't for you." He held onto the door handle, denting the metal in his hand while forcing his feet to stay put.

"Why impossible?"

"The yearnings you feel from mating would be uncontrollable without your mate to sustain them. If you were a shifter, you would already feel them to some extent, but once we mate, you will have the connection even as a human. It's a give and take when it comes to mating. There are advantages to it. The tradeoff is, you must deal with the demands of your body as well." He glanced down to find the door handle in his hand. Adam stepped toward her and held up the door handle. "I need a cold shower before I can't keep my desire in check anymore. My tiger wants you and it's tired of waiting."

"What happens to these yearnings if you die?"

"They would cease. When one mate dies, the mating is no longer active. The Elders say you will eventually find another mate. I prefer not to test their findings. Mating is an honor, we cherish and protect each other. Our numbers are lower, so mated couples are very important in order for our kind to continue."

She stood from the tub. Water flowed over her naked body and back down into the tub. "It's not very romantic, but we don't have a lot of time. Mate me. Make me yours."

"Do you know what you're asking?" He took a deep breath, breathing in her scent to see if her words were truly what she wanted. "I have control that many wish they had, and even I don't know if I can stop once we start. There is no going back. You need to be sure this is what you want."

She stepped out of the tub, not bothering to grab a towel. His shaft instantly hardened and he fought every instinct not to go to her, to bury his shaft deep within her until she screamed his name.

Robin smiled. "I've ignored my desire for you since you found me in Texas because I don't want to lose someone else I care about. I'm tired of running and living in fear. I want to enjoy life and being with you while I have you. I want you, this mating, and everything that goes with it…as long as you come back. Please don't go dying on me."

"Oh, I'll return to you." He scooped her up into his arms, his beast growling with anticipation as he turned to the bedroom. His beast craved her touch, as did he. Adam wanted to take advantage of each moment they had together before he had to leave. She wrapped her arms around his neck, pressing her wet body to his chest.

Laying her on the bed, he leaned over her, pressing his lips to hers. The warmth of her lips and the sweet scent of lavender from her bath mixed together to draw his tiger closer to the surface. He dragged his mouth from hers and kissed a path down her neck, breathing in her scent, imprinting it in his mind. Sensations collided and threatened to overwhelm him, but he pushed his beast away, savoring the moment—to have it last longer for her.

With his weight supported by his arms, inches above her, he met her gaze. "Are you sure? We will be connected in more ways than you imagine."

She stared at him while her hand slid down his side until she found his shaft. Her fingers wrapped around it and rubbed down the length, painstakingly slow. "I'm sure. Why fight what my body and heart want? I've only been bitchy about the whole situation, making the fact I'm surrounded by shifters an issue because I'm scared and tired of being alone. I don't want to lose anyone else I care about."

"You won't lose me." He dragged his tongue in lazy circles around her nipple. Teasing her nipples gently, he pulled them between his teeth until they stood at attention. He rested his weight on his elbow and used his other hand to explore the length of her body, memorizing every curve that would get him through the miles soon to separate them.

He blazed a hot, wet trail of kisses across her stomach, and stroked her thighs with his fingertips. With every touch, she arched her hips to him, demanding more. His desire soared to new heights, until he couldn't hold back any longer. Nudging her legs further apart with his knee, he cupped her hips, and delved his finger inside her. She met the teasing thrusts. He moved his hand and replaced it with his mouth. He pleased her with tiny nips and gentle licks over her sweet spot. She grabbed his hair with a mixture of pressing him closer and dragging him up.

"Adam, I need you."

Even with sexual haze driving him, he had enough control to take a moment to feel through her emotions, to make sure she would have no doubts later once lovemaking had completed their mating. "Your wish is my command, mate." He spread her legs further, giving him the access he needed. His control nearly maxed and he was thankful she was wet because he had no resistance left to go slow. He slid into her warm, wet core before sliding out and thrusting back in, his manhood filling her completely. The first few strokes were slow, but with each new stroke the tempo intensified another level until his hips where driving the force with each pump. His thrusts became deeper and faster, falling into a perfect rhythm. Their bodies rocked back and forth, tension stretching him tighter than a rubber band as he fought for the release he longed for.

She arched her body into his, her nails dug into his chest, and she screamed his name as her release arrived. He pumped twice more and growled her name as his released followed.

He stayed on top of her for a moment longer, watching the afterglow on her face and the ecstasy glossing her eyes. He then collapsed beside her, cradling her body tight against his as his fingers caressed her side. For the first time since he had found her, fear didn't course through her. He sensed contentment and love from her, making him want to hold her tighter.

Robin lay in Adam's embrace, feeling suddenly overwhelmed. She was experiencing so many emotions, she couldn't wrap her mind around it.

"What is it, love?" Adam's fingers teased her hip.

"I don't understand what's happening to me. It's like I'm in a funnel cloud and I can't make heads or tails of my emotions." Her panic rose. What did she get herself into?

"Give it time, it will calm, I promise. You're feeling me, my emotions, and my beast. Your body doesn't understand and is on overload at the moment, but in a few minutes the confusion will pass and you'll be able to comprehend the mating."

Minutes passed in a swirl of emotions until they finally died down as quickly as they came. Her muscles relaxed. "Will that come back?"

"No, you're human so the initial mating affects you differently at first. It overloads your body all at once, but now, if you focus, you'll be able to feel me. In time our connection will be second nature to you. You'll just know without focusing. You'll also now know I'm okay or uninjured. When I get to Virginia, there will be no reason for you to worry."

The thought of him going to Virginia made her tense again. It didn't matter how much he reassured her, she couldn't stop from worrying about him when he was going to face Pierce head on.

"I promise, I'll be back." He kissed the top of her forehead and snuggled her against his body.

"How can you promise something you have no control over?"

"Because I know the men I'm taking with me. We're a good team. I trust them to guard my back, as they trust me to do the same. With Ty going, we're taking triple the guards."

"Why is Ty going? If he's the Alpha, shouldn't he stay here, especially since you said Tabitha and him have to carry on the line for your kind to continue? Isn't it too much of a risk for him?"

"He's going to avenge the deaths of Tabitha's parents and Bethany's family. He sees it as his responsibility. Ty was living on the streets before Tabitha's father found him, helped him adjust to being a shifter, got him a job, a roof over his head, and a tutor because he couldn't attend school without risking exposure."

"Exposure? What happens to the children?"

"We have a school here at the compound, so our children are safe. If they shift, we don't have to worry about them exposing our nature, and if they can't shift, they can still attend the school here. You still okay with this?" He ruffled his fingers through her hair, drawing it away from her face.

Being able to feel his worry about her second thoughts, she kissed him, and then nodded as her lips hovered over his. "Yes, but not that I have a choice now. If Ty's going what about Raja?"

"Raja will stay here, protecting the mates and clan. I worked my way up the chain of command as one of Ty's guards, long before I became Tabitha's guard. It's another reason I have to be there to guard his back. I know it's hard to understand, this is new to you and you haven't seen us in a fight. We will be fine. I wouldn't take my Alpha into a fight that I thought we couldn't win. He's too important." His fingers slid down her body, exploring the curves of her hips.

She valued his courage and willingness to guard his Alpha. It showed his commitment to his clan and the cause they were fighting against, but his departure would also leave her alone in a new place and possibly alone forever. How could she fight him when she could feel how much it meant to him? *One night with my tiger isn't enough, he better come home to me.*

Chapter Nine

Hours later and another round of passionate love making, Adam's cell vibrated, alerting him to the gathering. He wanted to stay in bed with Robin's body pressed tightly against his, until the sun peeked through the blinds, but if he wanted to be part of the team, he needed to get to the meeting. Once the danger was eliminated, he'd be able to lay with her all day, and the fear running through her would be gone. "The meeting is in twenty minutes. Do you want to come?"

"Can I?" She leaned to look up at him.

"You gave us the information, so you're as much a part of this as I am. You don't have to go if you don't want to. When I receive the order to head out, I'll take you over to Raja and Bethany's quarters and get you settled before I leave."

"I understand why you have to go. I just still wish you weren't going."

He pressed his nose onto the top of her head, filling his senses with her scent. "I know. Stay here." He slid out of bed, and he pulled out a pair of blue jeans and black, long sleeve T-shirt from the dresser. Tugging his shirt over his head, he smiled. "I'm going outside, give me five minutes to get far enough away, and then focus on me. Think of whatever memory of me that brings me closest to you. It will make our connection easier. You'll feel me and know what I'm doing. The distance that separates us will be worse when I'm in Virginia or Boston, but you'll be able to know if I'm safe." He sat back on the bed, lacing his black, steel-toe boots.

"I thought we had to get ready for the meeting."

"We have a few minutes. You can get dressed while I'm gone. I want you to know how to make the connection, before I leave." He strapped his knife to his thigh strap before reaching for his gun and placing it in the holster on his hip. "It will become easier with practice." He leaned to kiss her and then closed the door behind him.

Adam glanced around the compound. This was his home. He'd fight for it with his dying breath. He just hoped the mission to eliminate Pierce wouldn't be his last, especially now that he found his mate. Jogging around the compound, he went to the far side of the property by the creek.

He stopped to watch the water flowing down the creek, feeling the cool air against his face, waiting for Robin's connection to spring to life. His life had gone full circle. A few years ago he stood next to a creek much like this one, searching for the rogue who took everything Adam had cherished. Now, here he was about to fight another rogue to protect his new future. He vowed to let nothing take what he held dear. He'd protect Robin, Tabitha, Ty, and the rest of the clan.

The wind sped past him, through him, cooling from the inside out as Robin's connection flared within him. The air's breeze held his mate's connection, yet allowed him to concentrate on whatever was at hand. Her force would be his strength when he was in a battle against Pierce. If the situation got out of control, and he didn't want Robin to sense what he was going through, there was a way to allow the shifter to dim the connection, as long as the other mate was human.

Hello Mate. He whispered through his thoughts, letting her know he could sense her.

Wow. Her voice crossed his mind as if she was right next to him. Her amazement tingled along his skin.

Now that you know how to communicate with me, meet me outside the cabin so we can go to the meeting. He would love to explore their bond more, but time was

76

limited. Turning, he headed toward his cabin. Their connection flickered as if she didn't want to give it up. She was probably afraid she might not be able to do it again. *Don't worry love, the second time is easier.*

With the goal of having Robin in his arms again, returning to the cabin seemed longer. He was proud that Robin was working with the mating abilities with such ease. Hopefully they would allow her to worry less while he was on the East Coast.

Robin ran to him at full speed. "I did it. I can't believe I did it." Excitement poured off her.

"I never doubted you." He wrapped his arms around her, drawing her tight against his chest and leaned to kiss her.

Robin sat next to Adam in the meeting, feeling somewhat out of place. This was Adam's life and if she was expecting to be a part of it she'd have to get used to these gatherings, but she hated sitting here while they planned to murder someone. The fact that Pierce had taken more lives than she could count helped a little. In the world she was raised in a man deserved a fair trial before being condemned. Adam, the Elders, and selected guards were acting like judge, jury, and executioner.

Ty waited until everyone was seated before starting. "A team from Jinx's West Virginia clan confirmed Pierce is in Virginia. He's alone as far as they can tell. They're standing guard until we get there or he tries to leave. Adam and I are going with a handful of other guards." He then explained what would happen in his absence. "Raja's in charge until I get back. Felix, I want you to take over the guest room in my quarters so you're always close by Tabitha while I'm gone. Two guards are to be on both Tabitha and Bethany at all times. Robin, you can stay with Bethany and her guards."

"Who is going to Virginia besides us?" Adam inquired.

"Taber, Styx, Marcus, as well as a few other ground guards. Galen is going to accompany us as a precaution. He won't be taking part in the mission, just close by in case he's needed. I don't want to take too many of our guards and leave the women unprotected. We'll be leaving within the hour. Taber is flying us to a nearby landing strip close to Pierce's location."

Over the next few minutes the game plan was laid out, covering each guard's duty. Robin only partially listened. She knew Adam and Styx would be with Ty, while Marcus would lead the other guards from the grounds. Other than that, she didn't care about the details. She only cared that Adam was putting himself at risk. There had to be another option? Something that would keep him safe.

"Why not just blow up the house?" The words flew out of her mouth before she had time to think. Showing just how much she wasn't paying attention, she assumed she must have interrupted an important conversation because everyone stared at her. "I'm sorry," she stuttered, wishing she hadn't opened her mouth.

"I like the way you think, and it's a good idea, but won't work." Ty smiled, making her more uneasy.

"Why won't it work? Can you guys survive an explosion?"

"Not necessarily. It would depend on the hit. Shifters have a better chance of survival than the average human, but there's a possibility we might die with everyone else from a direct explosion. We can't send in a bomb because Tabitha thinks there might be someone in the secret room she saw in Victor's memories. She's given me an idea of where the room is. Hopefully we get Pierce and find out who he is hiding." Ty wrapped his hand over Tabitha's. "She believes whoever is locked away is innocent. We can't blow up the area until we know if someone needs help."

"It's going to be okay." Adam rubbed Robin's thigh. "We have a plan and we're taking good men with us. We'll be fine."

She nodded. The determination in his eyes was not something she was willing to fight. She was unwilling to add any doubt in his mind. Her reservations might get him or others injured or worse. Because she wanted Adam and the others to return home safe, she decided to keep her mouth shut.

Ty leaned back in his chair, like the CEO of a high-powered firm, gazing around the room. "Adam, Styx, and Marcus, I want to go over more of the details with you privately. Everyone else can leave. Robin why don't you go with Bethany, she can show you were you'll stay until Adam returns. You shouldn't be at Adam's cabin alone in case there's an attack on the compound."

Adam leaned close to her side, his lips hovering just below her earlobe. His hot breath caressed her neck like a lover's touch. "It's okay, I'll come get you in a few."

With no option, she rose from her chair, following Bethany and her guards. Robin fought not to turn back to Adam. He was sensing what she was feeling, and he didn't need to see it in her eyes. Falling in pace with Bethany, they made their way out of the room and down the hall. Bethany turned to her.

"It's going to be all right. Adam is very skilled at what he does, so are the others."

Robin met Bethany's gaze. "Adam is Felix's second, as Styx is Shadow's. Why take both of the seconds from the guards? Shouldn't one of them stay here to protect you and Tabitha?"

"Styx is Shadow's second, more importantly he's also a very good warrior. Many would say he's vicious and kills without emotion. I've come to know Styx quite well since he's been assigned to my guard. I can tell you it's never without emotion. He's very good at what he does. They need him at their backs to take down Pierce. For a mission like this you only send the best, the ones you know will accomplish the job," Bethany explained.

"Makes sense, but I still don't like the plan. By everyone's omission, Pierce is dangerous. I can't believe I'm going to say this, but I wish they'd just kill him from afar." Her words made her wonder what kind of person this situation was turning her into. Working for a law office since graduation had proven to her time and time again that the legal system didn't always work the way people wanted, still she stood by it. Now here she was standing by while others took the law into their own hands. This wasn't who she was a few months ago. She wasn't sure what that said about her character, or about how much she could be influenced. Was this why people who lost loved ones killed the murderer, making them no better? An eye for an eye at the best or maybe worst. In the end, it left the whole world blind. Is that the type of world and people she wanted to surround herself with?

At that moment, hell yes. The Alaskan Tigers were the ones that would keep her alive. She cared about Adam and if that meant surrounding herself with animals that had animal beliefs, then she'd do it. Maybe this *was* a better world to live in long term. They fought for what they believed in and for the people they loved. The Alaskan Tigers were willing to take down a man who in her world would be considered a serial killer. Why did she have a problem with his demise? Especially when there was no doubt he'd kill again. Pierce didn't just limit his kills to shifters, he killed without discretion, putting everyone in danger.

The realization that bothered her most about the situation was that Adam was placing himself at risk while she sat in safety, waiting for him to return. Would she have to deal with this every time there was a threat to his clan, or shifters? Adam was certainly the man she wanted by her side if something happened, but could she stand by with him leaving her time after time to keep innocents safe? She didn't have an answer. Instead she promised that once they got through the Pierce situation she'd revaluate it. Would it be too late for her to change her mind since they had consummated the mating? Surely if she had second thoughts, she could get out of it. There had to be a shifter divorce or something, right?

Tex strolled toward them, his eyes holding a haunting look. He seemed to look right past everyone. "Tex?" She called out to him, barely catching a glimpse from him. It was like he was in a drug-induced state. "Bethany, I've got to talk to Tex. You go ahead. I'll find you or Adam later. This can't wait."

"Jayden stay with her, and bring her to the quarters when she's done," Shadow ordered, placing her hand on Bethany's back to keep her moving down the hall. "Drew and I will take Bethany home now."

"I don't need anyone to guard me." Robin argued.

"You're still in danger until Pierce is eliminated. Jayden will stay with you for now," Shadow hollered over her shoulder.

"We better follow Tex if you want to speak with him. I'm not sure where the Elders have put him," Jayden said as Robin looked at the backs of Bethany and her guards.

Robin felt torn. In the end speaking to Tex won out. "Tex, wait." She jogged after him, picking up her pace when he didn't stop. Jayden fell into step next to her, leaving it evident he could have over taken her if he wasn't guarding her.

Finally catching up to Tex, she placed her hand on his arm to stop him. He swung toward her, growls erupting from him, and his hand rose as if to strike her. He would have hit her if Jayden hadn't been there to grab Tex's arm in mid-swing.

"What the hell are you thinking man? Are you on something?" Jayden's words seemed to awaken Tex.

Tex stood ridged as Jayden stood between them. "What do you want? I don't know either of you. How do you know my name?"

All her years working with angry people, grieving spouses for their marriage, and just downright rude people, Robin had developed a way of mixing sympathy and authority in her tone. She used her skill on Tex, hoping to keep him calm. She didn't need him to lose it again. Jayden might not be quick enough to intervene. "Tex, I was in Texas the night you were injured. I was the woman with Adam. We didn't officially meet since you were unconscious. Do you have a few minutes? I'd like to talk to you."

When Tex didn't say anything, Jayden spoke. "The compound's main kitchen is just down the hall. We could grab some coffee and talk. It should be empty this time of day."

"Sound good, Tex?" She strolled toward the area, hoping he'd follow.

"Okay." He followed her and once they were in the kitchen they each grabbed some coffee before making their way to a table.

"I'll be right here, Tex, don't do anything stupid," Jayden warned, sitting down a few tables away.

From what Adam told her, Jayden would still be able to hear her conversation with Tex. At least it gave them the idea of privacy. After Tex's outburst she was thankful to have Jayden with her. She knew she stood no chance against a shifter, but with Jayden close at least she wouldn't be killed by a spooked and abused tiger.

"Tex, what I want to talk to you about isn't an easy subject. You don't have to say anything if you don't want to. I only want to say my peace." She paused, taking a sip. The rich spiced aroma and taste of expensive coffee filled her. Oh how she missed good cup of joe during her time on the run. The motels and restaurants she visited, while in hiding, had cheap and sometimes downright awful coffee. She leaned back against the chair, enjoying the rush of strong caffeine raging through her system, before turning her attention back to Tex.

"Adam brought you here not only because of your injuries, but because

82

he believes you were abused." He started to say something and she held up her hand. She didn't want him to lie or to deny the beatings. "I'm not asking for you to confirm it, or even deny it to save your pride, just hear me out."

He looked down at the table, his hands wrapped around the coffee mug as if soaking up the heat it offered. The warmth he was seeking couldn't be found from the coffee mug. He needed people that cared for what he sought.

"I've worked with many woman and children who have been abused, even a few men. Sadly it's rare for them to want to share their experiences, or even talk to a woman. More importantly, I've been in your shoes. The signs are clear as the circles under your eyes when I look at you, and the way you reacted to my approach in the hall. Adam gave you a choice by bringing you here, and I understand that you can stay here if you choose. We're not supposed to influence you and I'm not trying to. All I'm asking is for you to think about the life you could have, without fear before you make a decision."

She leaned forward, keeping her voice low. "Your last words before you became unconscious were that your Alpha would see it as failure and you didn't want to die. Make the decision to live—without being abused, or under anyone's thumb. You're young and deserve a chance to experience life."

"How do you know? What if there isn't any different?" He paused, shaking his head. His short blonde hair peaked out from under his cowboy hat.

"I know because my former husband beat the crap out of me anytime he was pissed. Any bad business decision he made, I suffered. It didn't matter the reason, he'd find an excuse to make it my fault, just to knock me around a few times. He said it put me in my place. He used me as his punching bag. I don't want to see you or anyone else in that situation." She sat her coffee mug aside and moved her chair closer. She saw Jayden tense a little as if waiting for Tex to react, but Tex stayed calm. "Adam found me in Texas just hours before coming to that landing strip. He brought you here because of what was happening to you in Texas. He wouldn't have brought you from one bad situation to another. Adam isn't that type of man."

"What if Avery comes after me?" His tone was fearful. The glare in his eyes was as if he dared Avery to come after him.

"The Alaskan Tigers stick together, they fight for each other and those who can't fight for themselves. I know for a fact that if you choose not to go back to Texas they will stand by your side. Give your commitment to Ty and the Alaskan Tigers and you won't have to worry. Avery wouldn't dare take them on. Look at Pierce, he's sending his people to do the dirty work because he's too scared to come after them head on. Avery is no different. Abusers are cowards. You have my word if you stay here you'll be protected. No one will hurt you."

"How can you make that promise? You're not one of them."

She gave him a huge smile. "My mate is and his word is gold. Come with me and I'll prove it, but only if you're serious about staying here. The Elders are busy and I don't want to interrupt them if you have no intention on staying."

"I want to stay. I'm just concerned if Avery comes here he'll not only kill me, but he'll blame them for keeping me here. I don't want to see anyone else fall into Avery's hands."

She rose, holding out her hand. "Come with me, we'll get their word and you'll be safe. I'll be here as well and can make sure nothing happens."

He shook his head again, fear returning to his eyes. "You're human. You wouldn't survive his…games."

"I have no intentions on that. I meant that you'll be safe here. I'll see to it. I suspect now that they know he's abusing his clan, they will do something about it, but that isn't my place to guess. Right now they are dealing with Pierce. They must eliminate him before he kills any others." She still had her hand out, waiting for him to take it.

When he slid his hand into hers, she wanted to scream with excitement. To know she saved someone from the hands of an abuser sent joy through her. She prayed Adam and his Elders would hold up the bargain she made for Tex. It wasn't as if she did it without knowing them and their ways. Adam had informed her of his clan's protection of each other when she agreed to come to Alaska.

Chapter Ten

Adam leaned back in the conference room chair mildly amused, watching Tabitha and Ty fight amongst themselves. Tabitha wanted to go after Pierce and obviously Ty was against it. Styx, Marcus, and Adam watched, hoping they wouldn't have to take sides.

"Damn it, Ty, I told you in Pittsburgh I wanted to go after him."

"Yeah you told me. That doesn't mean I was going to let you. If you remember I just let that comment fall to the side. It was pointless to argue with you then, especially when I knew we'd be having this conversation again when the time came. The answer is no, you're not going. You're too important to the tigers to let you go off risking your safety. You're too important to me. I can't focus on what needs to be done if I'm worrying about your safety. You're staying here." Ty stood his ground even under Tabitha's intense stare.

"What? And you're not important to the clan, to the tigers? I can't do what I need to without you by my side." Tabitha wasn't giving up without a fight and she didn't seem to care there was an audience.

"Nothing is going to happen to me. I have the skills to protect myself and I have these men at my back. We're going to be fine. I need you here to help Raja keep the rest of the clan calm."

Adam couldn't help the smile that tugged at the corner of his lips. His Alpha was digging a hole deeper and deeper with each statement. He had fought against Tabitha in the practice ring and knew she was as fierce as some male guards. She could hold her own in a fight and her shooting accuracy was unbelievable.

"Are you saying I don't have the skills to protect myself? What about all the hours that Bethany and I have been putting in with the guards learning hand to hand combat, and the hours at the range learning to shoot without missing? I can handle myself."

Ty let out a deep breath as if tired of the fight. "Damn it, Tabby, you know that's not what I'm saying. I know how good you are, but damn it, I want you here—safe. This job is my responsibility. I will see that Pierce pays for the people he killed."

"He killed my parents, and I want to see him dead for it. That's my right. Don't deny me."

Ty gripped the back of the chair, his knuckles turning white. "I'm doing this for you. Hell, next you're going to say Bethany should go because he killed her parents and sister too. I'm not taking women into the field with me, not on this."

"So this isn't because I'm not as good as you and the guards, but because I don't have a dick?" Tabitha's anger soared off the charts.

Adam pushed away from the table. Someone had to put an end to this fight if they were going to get to Virginia before Pierce realized they were watching his house and made a move. "Stop it, you two. We don't have time for this. If anyone in this room is going to avenge the deaths of Bethany and your families then we need to get on the plane." He sighed. "Tabitha, you're exceptional in practice, but it's different than going on a mission. Styx and I need to be focused on keeping Ty safe. We aren't taking enough guards to guarantee your safety as well. I agree with Ty, you need to stay here. We need you here in case there's an attack." Suddenly both of his Alphas were staring at him, and for the briefest second he wondered if he should have kept his mouth shut.

It was Tabitha who spoke first, breaking the unease. "You're right,

Adam. It shouldn't matter who takes Pierce down as long as he's no longer a problem. I won't force you to take me with you because it will only hinder what you're doing there. I will tell you this though, if any of you get hurt there's going to be hell to pay when you get back."

Adam nodded, relieved that Tabitha had decided they were wasting precious time. "We'll protect Ty with our lives you know that."

"No, protect each other. Watch each other's backs. I don't want any of you injured or worse." Tabitha slid her arms around Ty's waist. "You are all my family, I love each of you."

"We'll be fine, love." Ty snuggled her close and kissed the top of her head.

As Adam watched, he hoped Robin and him would eventually have such a strong mating bond, where she could be as understanding of his job as Tabitha was for Ty. Only time would tell.

A knock on the door put his head in overdrive. He could sense his mate with two males. Rising, he went to the door, standing in the middle so he'd blocked Ty and Tabitha when he opened it. It didn't matter who was behind the door, it was his job to protect his Elders. Months ago, they learned of a traitor in the midst of the compound. They had to be vigilant it wouldn't happen again. Instead of coming to his Elders to seek help, Chris betrayed his clan to save his sister from Pierce.

"Adam, I know you're busy, but Tex…he needs some assurance before you leave," Robin explained why she interrupted the meeting.

"What have you done? I told you we were not to influence his decision." Adam looked from his mate to Tex.

"I didn't. I saw him on my way to Bethany's. Jayden accompanied me while I spoke with Tex."

"The decision to stay in Alaska or go back to Texas must be his and his alone." Ty stepped next to Adam.

"Sir, the decision would be mine. Robin and I were only talking about my options. I didn't mean to get her in any trouble." Tex drew the attention away from Robin. It was both honorable and stupid, depending on the situation.

"Come inside, let's not talk about this in the hall." Ty stepped aside, let them in the room, and closed the door behind them. "What is it that you want reassurance on?"

When Tex didn't speak, Robin answered for him. "Go over what happens if he stays. He's concerned Avery will bring trouble upon your clan."

"I'm sure Tabitha and I could handle this once you and the others have gotten safely on your way," Raja told Ty.

Ty nodded. "That's true. Tex, all of your questions and concerns can be answered by Raja and Tabitha, if you can give us a bit of time. The rest of us are gearing up for a mission."

"If you could just tell him he would be safe here, that you won't turn him over to Avery, I believe that will help him greatly," Robin urged.

"Robin, this is not the time." Adam stared at her, trying to get a message across that Tex's situation needed to be dealt with later.

Tex turned to leave, but Ty stopped him. "We won't turn you over to Avery as long as staying here is your decision. I hope Robin is not influencing you to stay because if you wish to remain here giving your commitment to my Lieutenant Raja and my mate is the same as giving it to me. Raja and Tabitha will answer any of your questions and set you up in a long term cabin. Then they'll discuss what you can contribute to the clan."

"It's my decision to remain here, sir. I'll let you get back to your meeting. If I could have a word with your Lieutenant later, I'd appreciate it." Tex turned to the door. "Come on, Robin, let's let them get back to what they were doing. We shouldn't have bothered them."

"I'll send for you after this meeting has finished, and we can then discuss your situation," Raja told Tex.

Robin looked to Adam as if she wanted to say something, but then followed Tex out. "Robin, we're almost done. I'll find you in a few minutes and we can gather your belongings to take them to Bethany's."

When the door clicked shut behind Robin, Adam turned to Ty. "I apologize for my mate. The human world works different than how it runs for shifters."

Ty waved his hand. "There's no need to apologize. Tex is young and scared, and Robin is trying to help him. That's very honorable of her. Now we've got to get a move on. See your mate settled and meet the team at the landing strip in twenty minutes."

Leaving the conference room, Adam followed Robin's scent down the hall to the cafeteria and found her sitting with Tex, Jayden standing nearby. It seemed slightly odd to see his mate with a guard normally reserved for the Elder's mates. Thankfully, unlike Tabitha and Bethany, it was not something he would have to deal with long. Jayden protecting Robin was just a precaution until the mission to eliminate Pierce was complete. Robin was on Pierce's list along with Tabitha and Bethany, there was no way Adam would deny his mate the additional protection especially with him heading to Virginia.

"Love, we need to get your things and then I can show you where you'll be staying while I'm gone." He stood next to his mate.

Tex rose from his chair, holding out his hand. "I just want to thank you for saving my skin in Texas."

"There's no need. Even if your situation was different I wouldn't have left you there to die." Adam took his hand, shaking it. "I just hope my mate hasn't pushed you into any decision that isn't your own. This clan is nothing like the one you've come from. We're a family here, we don't force people to do what we want, nor do we abuse people."

91

"I want to stay, but what if Avery comes here? I don't want to bring danger to your clan."

Adam laid his hand on Robin's shoulder. "I doubt he'll come here, either way Avery needs to be dealt with once this mission is over. We can't stand by letting him abuse his clan. The coming months will be a change for a number of clans, not just the Texas Tigers. If you could excuse us, I need a few minutes with my mate before I leave."

Tex nodded. "Very well. Thank you, Robin. I'll see you again."

"If you need anything let me know, or if you want to talk," Robin told Tex as he left.

Her words sent a strange twinge of jealousy through Adam. He shouldn't be upset that she wanted to help the kid, but he didn't like the idea of Tex seeing more of his mate over the next few days when he was gone. He wanted to take advantage of every moment they had together, but there was too much to do. "Jayden, you can return to your duties. I'll bring Robin to Bethany's."

"Yes, sir." Jayden nodded and headed down the hall to his post.

Robin stood, straightening her yellow sweater. "Why do I feel that you're upset that I offered to help Tex?"

"Not upset, just wishing it was me you'd be spending the coming days with. I can think of a number of things we could do to pass the hours." He didn't mention that if she kept walking in on Elders' meetings it was going to start reflecting badly on him. His mate's actions could cause issues with his position. This time it had been for a good cause, but next time, well, he didn't know. They'd have to wait to see how things went in the coming months. If she didn't take to the tiger's way of life then they would have to have a serious talk.

"According to you, we will have lots of time once you return, so why worry that I'm helping Tex?"

"You're right, there's no reason to envy. A shifter's jealousy isn't for the same reason humans feel it. Once you've mated, the sexual contact from another is painful. There is no fear of cheating among our kind." He reached out, taking her hand. "Now, come along, we don't have a lot of time and I'd like to have you settled before I leave."

She accepted his hand, but didn't move from where she was standing. "Even if that wasn't the case, I'm not that kind of woman. I would never cheat on someone I'm in a relationship with."

"I didn't mean to imply you were, only that it wasn't the reason you felt my jealousy. I was merely trying to explain the ways of my kind." He was tired of the division between them. He'd always be a tiger, while she'd always be human. How were they to get past it? Feeling through her emotions, he searched to see if she still had doubts in her thoughts, and came up with nothing. Was she finally thinking of him as her mate instead of as a tiger?

Chapter Eleven

Robin had hoped to see Adam off at the landing strip with the others until Tabitha asked if she'd accompany her and Raja to meet with Tex. Having already formed a friendship of sorts with Tex, even if it was only based on their abused pasts, would put him more at ease with her present.

Tabitha pulled her aside while they waited for Raja to join them. "I'm so glad Adam found you. He's an amazing man. He'll give you the world and make you happy if you allow him."

Pushing her hair away from her face, Robin frowned. "I'm wondering how I'm going to get a normal life back being with him. Not because he's a tiger, it's just I lost so much. What will I do with my degree and work experience here?"

"You worked with a law firm, if I remember correct, before all this. You can still do that. Well, hopefully not with the one in Virginia because we'd hate to see you leave. Telecommunication is an option. The law firms here aren't nearly as high powered as what you're used to or even as busy, still you might be able to find work with them. We don't have a lot of legal work, but we do have a lawyer in the clan. He is retired from normal practice and only handles the clan's legal business. I'm sure he'd appreciate the help. There are also other jobs you might be interested in around the compound. You have a lot of options."

Robin wanted to complain about everything she had lost, not just her job, but how could she complain to Tabitha when she had lost so much more, and still made a life here with Ty. From what Adam told her, Tabitha had stepped into this new life and her role as the Queen of the Tigers without any hesitation.

Felix joined them before Robin had time to figure out how to respond to Tabitha. "Raja said he'd meet us there. He wants us to go ahead and ease Tex's fears before he shows up. Korbin is in the hall. He'll stand in as your other guard, Tabitha, while Adam is away. Thomas has some other commitments to deal with, so he'll be with me from time to time."

"Very well. Let's go see what Tex wants to do, and then we'll have an idea what to say if Avery calls us again. Hopefully the men will be back before Avery makes any sort of challenge. It all depends on how much Tex really means to him. I doubt much since he's been so badly abused. How can you claim to care for someone if you abuse them?" Tabitha shook her head, and led the way to the door.

"For some it's a learned trait. Many abusers can only show love with their fits. I've seen the turnaround if the abuser finds another source for their anger." She couldn't stop from explaining, even if Tabitha wasn't interested.

"How do you know so much about abuse?" Felix inquired as they made their way down the hall—Korbin in front, with Tabitha and Robin in the middle, and Felix bringing up the rear.

"I spent years in an abused spouse group, trying to gather the courage to leave Bobby. I had saved the money and was ready to leave when Bobby was killed." She took a deep breath, trying not to remember the big plans she had. "I helped other people get away from their abusive spouses, counseled them when they needed, and was overall a friendly shoulder to cry on. The group never knew I was in the same situation because I didn't want it getting back to my law firm since they were the ones who started the group for their clients. The group saved me. I only hoped I helped others."

"I think we've found your calling for the clan." Tabitha glanced at her.

"What do you mean?" Robin was puzzled by what any of her past had to do with how she was going to contribute to the clan.

"Taking Avery out of his position of power over the Texas Tigers is going to leave a lot of abused shifters needing counseling. You can help with their transition. Teach them the tricks you learned and help them work through it. I've never experienced abuse so I don't understand what they are going through. No offense meant. I just can't understand why they stay." There was sadness in Tabitha's eyes.

"Some stay because they don't think they can make it on their own. Others, like Tex, fear for their lives. I stayed because Bobby was all I had and I loved him. To this day a part of me still loves the man he was when we married. It wasn't until later that he became abusive. At first I made excuses for him. The bruises were always hidden so others couldn't see them." They walked in silence for a few minutes as if Tabitha took in everything Robin said.

"I think you might be able to help with Harmony. She's been on her own most of her life before Ty and Raja found her staggering in the woods. Her leg got caught in a bear trap, now she's so scared around people she won't shift back." Tabitha stopped outside one of the doors.

"I don't know how I can help if she's in tiger form. Do you even understand people when you're in your other form?"

Tabitha nodded. "We comprehend everything. I've listened to her thoughts and have learned what makes her scared. There's nothing I can do to help her heal from what she's been through. Once we finish with Tex, we can go see Harmony this evening, if you're up to it?"

A warm glow filled Robin with the thought of giving back to the people that were giving her so much. She couldn't stay here unless she found a way to contribute. Adam was an important part of the clan and she couldn't sit around doing nothing. If she could help the clan by assisting with the abused, then she'd do it no questions asked.

Tabitha knocked on the door. "Tex, it's Tabitha, Alpha Female for the Alaskan Tigers, I need to speak with you."

The solid wood door swung open. Tex stood there in his jeans, the T-shirt he had on earlier and his cowboy hat both gone. The scars Robin saw during the helicopter ride from Texas were displayed for all to see. His muscles made it clear he put in serious hours at the gym. They gave him a manly appearance to go with his youthful face. Without the cowboy hat he appeared even younger than his twenty-four. Adam mentioned shifters aged slower, which is why Tex looked so young. While his eyes said he had seen a lot in his years, most of that had been at the hands of Avery.

"Tabitha is here to speak with you about joining the clan. Can we come in?" Robin asked when he continued to block the doorway, his gaze gliding over each of the guards. "Felix and Korbin are here for Tabitha's protection, they mean you no harm. You should be aware the Elder mates have guards," she added, trying to keep him calm.

"Come in." He stepped aside, allowing her, Tabitha, and Felix to enter. Korbin stayed outside the door watching the hall.

"Thank you, Tex," Tabitha said. "Raja will be joining us shortly, until then, what can I do to help you. If you wish to go back to Texas we can arrange that, or if you wish to remain here we will take the steps to make that happen." Tabitha moved into the room and toward the small living area with a sofa and chair.

"I'd like to stay if you can assure me I'd have a home here. Texas has been my home and if I give it up to stay here, I won't be welcomed back. I don't want the life of solitude." Tex lowered onto the chair.

Tabitha nodded, sitting further away from him as if not to spook him. "You would have a home as long as you bring no harm to my clan, or anyone that is protected by us. That includes the Kodiak Bears and West Virginia Tigers. They are our partners and deserve the same respect."

He leaned against the chair, slouching his shoulders in defeat. "Avery will take grave offense to this. He might attack your clan. I could be jeopardizing your clan."

"That would not be your fault. Avery is a grown man and makes his own decisions. Whether he brings the fight to us or we take it to him, there will be changes to the Texas Tigers. You need to decide which side of the fight you want to be on. We can't let Avery continue as he has been. This would be the time to join our clan if you wish, not later." Tabitha looked away from Tex as the door opened and Raja stepped in.

"I feel bad about drawing your clan into this. This was a fight the Texas Tigers should have dealt with long ago, but most of them are in the same position as I am. Avery rules his state with his fists, there's no respect for him, just fear." Tex ran his hand through his hair, the blond hair was cut so short it spiked on its own.

Tabitha glanced to Raja who nodded before she turned her attention back to Tex. "Avery is going to be a worry of the past soon. Do we have your word you will put the Alaskan Tigers before any commitments you have to anyone else? That you will protect our clan and not share any information with anyone other than those who are members of the clan? That you will speak with me, Raja, or Ty if for some reason you feel you are unable to do your duties?"

"You should also know that if you betray this clan in any way you would be forfeiting your life. We do not take kindly to traitors." Raja stated from just beyond the living area.

"I understand and you have my word. Whatever you need from me, I'll do. I just don't want to live like that any longer. I was a guard for Avery so if you need assistance with guards I would gladly help." Tex looked between Tabitha and Raja before moving his gaze to Robin. "Thank you, for finding me this morning. I wasn't sure what to do. I was so lost, pulled in two different directions and not wanting anyone else to get hurt because of my actions."

"You're welcome. Knowing what you were going through, at least partially, I had to at least try." Robin squeezed his hand for reassurance.

"If you want to come on as a guard, we'll start you on ground duty to see how you do. But before you begin, I want you to talk to Robin or Doc. We need to know you're fit for duty. Robin might be able to help you. She has experience with this act of violence. If you prefer to talk to Doc, I know he will make the time. Whatever you say to them would be confidential. They would only tell me if you're capable of protecting the clan, and provide me with an honest opinion on your mental state," Tabitha added.

"I don't…"

Tabitha held up her hand, stopping him. "Until this session is complete you won't be guarding anyone, nor will you receive your weapons back. I have to think of the safety of the clan, and you've been through a lot, so reassurance is a necessity."

"If there's someone else besides Robin or Doc you'd feel more comfortable speaking with we could see about making arrangements." Raja stepped closer.

Tex nodded, accepting their conditions. "I'll talk with Robin, if that's fine with her."

When Raja and Tabitha looked at Robin, she smiled. "That's fine." How could she say no to Tex when she understood what he was going through? He would be her first introduction to working with more cases in the future. She should have gone to college to study counseling instead of legal studies.

Chapter Twelve

Adam sat on a swivel chair. Normally when he travelled he flew the helicopter, this was his first time in the private plane the Alaskan Tigers owned. For once it was enjoyable to sit back and relax while Taber flew them to Virginia.

"It's going to be late night when we finally make it to Pierce's location, swinging the favor toward us," Ty explained, looking at the email Jinx's guards sent. "Weres are not able to see as well as full-blooded shifters at night. With even more luck maybe Pierce will be sleeping and our mission will go off without a hitch."

"My men also advised that he's alone. There are no guards protecting him." Jinx swiveled in his chair.

Adam was only slightly surprised to find out Jinx would be accompanying them on the mission. Taking down Pierce affected all tiger shifters, but it had been the Alaskan Tigers fight since nearly the beginning. Jinx's clan recently joined a partnership with the Alaskan Tigers, bringing the clans as one unit.

Taber's voice cracked through the overhead speaker. "I've received confirmation my brothers are airborne. They should be arriving thirty minutes behind us in Virginia."

Adam pressed the button connecting them to the cockpit. "Additional support is even better. Who's coming, Taber?"

"Theodore and the twins, Turi and Trey." Taber was one of the eldest twins next in line to lead the Kodiak Bears when their father stepped down.

They were the best fighters of the group, but none of the Bears were slackers in that department.

"We have more than enough men even if this mission goes off track." The eagerness coming off Ty tingled in the air. "Marcus you're leading the other group, focus on finding the room. If possible, Pierce is mine. I'd love to see him suffer for all the pain he's caused, but we're better than that. I want him to look into my eyes and know I'm going to kill him. The kill will be as humane as possible. I will not stoop to his level no matter how tempting it would be."

"We'll take Taber with us." Adam leaned his head against the soft leather seat. "Marcus you'll take Turi and Trey with you. Pick one guard to stay with Theodore and keep guard outside. Make sure no one else approaches. I suggest everyone get a little rest before we arrive. It could be a long night."

Adam let his eyelids fall shut, not in search of sleep, but for the connection with Robin. His eyes didn't need to be closed for the connection, it only allowed for him to forget about the distance between them. The connection tingled along his skin as he felt Robin reaching out to him. Her longing for him and her fear became stronger with their connection. It matched his desire to hold her in his arms again.

Through their connection he could tell what she was doing, thinking, and feeling. It was almost as if he was there with her. What surprised him was how she was adjusting to clan life. He saw her comfortably chatting with the Elder mates, Tabitha and Bethany. The woman had formed a plan to help the newest female member of the clan, Harmony. Everything was working out better than he hoped. Now all he had to do was to make it back to her. He wanted to feel her body against his, her lips on his, and her fingers teasing along his chest as they cuddled. He was missing her more than he thought. It was true that one didn't truly understand mating until they had consummated the relationship. Maybe they wouldn't have an uphill battle while she tried to find her place.

Robin and the Elder mates had devised a plan for her to speak with Harmony after dinner. The compound might have been a safe haven so far, but when someone new stepped into Tabitha's quarters, Robin couldn't stop the tension from rising. Setting her coffee aside, she held tight to the connection Adam brought to life a short time before. His calming nature smoothed over her like running water.

They are friendly. Taber's brother, Thorben, and their mate, Kallie. You're safe, I swear. Adam whispered through their connection.

With nearly fifty clan members Robin had to get used to meeting new people or she was going to have a nervous breakdown.

"Korbin let us in," Kallie explained, coming around to sit next to Tabitha on the sofa. Thorben stood by the side of the sofa, acting more like a bodyguard than a mate. "I wanted to find out how Harmony was and if I could do anything."

Bethany must have caught Robin eyeing Thorben because she leaned closer to Robin. "If you're looking for differences between the twins don't bother. Kallie swears they are different, though we can't see it. They act like her personal bodyguards, but on rare occasions you will see a loving side to them."

"It's not rare." Kallie defended before she reached up and slid her hand into her mates. "They give me everything I need and I tell you there are differences. Robin you'll just have to see them side by side and I'll show you. Taber is on the mission with the others, but I'll show you when he's back. You'll see, I'm not making it up."

Tabitha and Bethany laughed, as if they had heard it all before. Tabitha gained control of herself, smiling at Kallie she added. "Side by side and Robin will still not see these differences you find. The only ones I've seen are in their personality and those are minuscule."

The easy relationship between these women had Robin longing to be part of it. If she agreed to help the abused shifters, she'd be working more with Tabitha and Bethany. This connection would hopefully give her the same relationship that Kallie had with them.

"Fine." Kallie let out a puff of air as if she was offended they didn't believe her but the smile that lite up her face made it clear she wasn't angry. "What's going on with Harmony?"

"I'm taking Robin over there after dinner. She's going to help me talk to her. Maybe we will make more progress," Tabitha told Kallie.

"Who's going with you? Adam is gone and Felix scares Harmony so you're without your main guards." Thorben eyed Tabitha with concern.

"Raja will be with us and Felix and Korbin will be outside. It was the only way the men would agree without Ty here. There's nothing to worry about. Harmony is scared, but is coming around." Tabitha smiled.

"I can come with you," Thorben said. "I'm sure Kallie could stay with Bethany while I was there or I can have someone else watch over her."

Kallie looked up at her mate. "The compound is safe, I don't need you or Taber with me at all times. You know, I did just fine before we mated."

Thorben leaned down, kissing her. "I know, but it's our duty to protect you. You've been blessed with not one but two mates, so you never get rid of one of us, you know that."

"It's hard enough getting rid of one." Bethany laughed, turning slightly in her chair to glance at Raja who was working on his laptop a few feet away. "It must be nearly impossible to get rid of two."

"It's beyond impossible. I don't think I've been alone since I've mated." Kallie cuddled into Thorben.

"It's what happens when you mate a shifter. We cling to our mates with our claws," Raja added without even looking up from his laptop.

Talking about mates made Robin miss Adam even more. She had only known him a short time and yet she couldn't picture her life without him. He wasn't just her safety and security anymore, she was actually falling in love with him. *He might get killed on this mission and I didn't tell him how I feel.*

Chapter Thirteen

Stepping out into the open air Robin tipped her head back, letting the cool evening air caress her face, and blow her hair away from her face, tangling it. Aurora Borealis lit up the sky—the blues, greens, and pinks mixing together formed a beautiful sky.

"They're impressive aren't they?" Tabitha stood beside Robin watching the sky, while Raja, Felix, and Korbin kept guard, watching the grounds for anything unusual.

"I've never seen anything like that. It's amazing." No words could describe what Robin saw in the sky. It seemed perfect. She knew there was a scientific reason for the lights, serving to remind her that she was a mere small piece of the whole picture. Maybe her puzzle piece fit into the Alaskan Tigers' clan.

Raja cleared his throat, drawing her attention. "Ladies, I'd like to get back to the main compound before the team lands in Virginia, so if we could carry on."

Nodding, Robin followed his lead. Her thoughts turned to the change in her attitude since she arrived. When Adam first landed the helicopter and Ty and Raja waited for them, she was intimidated. Her heart raced in her ears and she wanted to scream for Adam to fly away. Now that she had spent time with the Elders, she realized they meant no harm to her.

Would the world know about the Alaskan Tigers and shifters in general one day? She wasn't sure the world was ready, but each day slowly moving forward and within a few years maybe they could live side by side without fearing the unknown. For now, she was honored to be a part of their close-knit clan.

Harmony stayed in one of the studio apartments some of the single members and guards lived in. The only difference, she had a guard at her door to guarantee no one bothered her and that she didn't run off before she was healed.

"Evening, Lance," Raja called to the guard stationed outside the door. "Take a twenty minute break, go get something to eat or a coffee."

"Yes, Sir." Lance nodded and strolled off.

"Ready?" Raja asked Robin and Tabitha and opened the door. Felix and Korbin took their post on each side of the door. If something should happen, they were close enough to defend their Lieutenant and get the women to safety. When Raja and the women entered, Harmony jumped off the bed, scurrying to the side out of direct view.

"Harmony, I brought a friend with me, her name is Robin." Tabitha moved closer to the bed so she could see the tigress, still keeping Raja a step in front of her. The rules were clear, they were to get no closer than Raja.

"Can she understand us in her animal form?" Robin asked, coming to stand on the other side of Tabitha.

"She hears you, she just can't talk in that form. I can hear her thoughts."

"Harmony, I'm sure you've smelled that I'm human. I joined the clan recently, so I know you're scared. The Elders and this situation can be intimidating." Robin paused, trying to figure out the best way to approach the woman. It would have been easier if she could get a feel for Harmony, but in her tigress form Robin couldn't get a read on Harmony's emotions. She wasn't growling, did that mean she wasn't angry? Or was she waiting to pounce?

Biting the bullet, Robin met the gaze of the tigress. "I know what you went through in Ohio. I can help you work through it. I've been in a similar

108

circumstance. The fear you hold inside is like water on the stove boiling over."

"Keep going, you're getting through to her," Tabitha whispered.

"You have two choices, let it control you or you control it. I chose to grab it by the reins and get my life back. You can too. I can help if you shift. The person you fear won't get to you as long as you remain here. The Elders and guards will see to that. Shift back and let us help you. At least give it a try and we'll go from there." Robin prayed she was getting through to the young woman.

The tigress rose and Robin thought she might attack. The reddish-orange and black hair slowly sank into Harmony's skin. Bones seemed to break and morph into different shapes as she stood on two feet. In a matter of seconds, she went from being seven feet long from head to tail and over three hundred pounds, to standing naked and no more than ninety pounds. Her skin was unhealthy pale—almost translucent. Her ruby red hair and freckles only enhanced her pastiness.

Raja stepped forward, reaching for a blanket. Harmony pressed up against the wall. "Here." He handed her the blanket without moving closer to her. A timid hand reached out, taking the blanket from his outstretched hand.

"Why don't you get dressed before we talk?" Tabitha motioned toward the small hallway and opened bathroom door. "The clothes from your bag were washed and are hanging in the closet." Tabitha and Robin went to sit on the sofa and chair in the sitting area.

The studio apartments were small, with everything to make it homey. Eventually, each member of the clan would receive their own cabin. The priority went to married members, then the top Elder guards, before moving down to the rest of the clan members.

Tabitha offered Robin to take the corner seat, closer to the chair where Harmony would sit when she joined them. "I knew you would be great at this. You were able to get through to her, when the rest of us couldn't."

"I'm not sure it was me. Maybe she was just tired of feeling trapped. Either way, I'm glad she did. I'll work with her as much as she wants, but I'm not a licensed councilor. She might need more help than I can give her."

"I know you were one semester away from your master's degree in psychology." Tabitha nudged her. "You're the best we have. She can't talk to someone who doesn't know that shifters exist. Have you thought about going back for your last semester? It could be beneficial to have a licensed therapist on our team."

"I took the college classes because I was working with so many people who needed support, as well as the abused spouses group. Bobby hated my studies and tried to force me to quit. It was my first real rebellion from his rule when I continued in school. If he wouldn't have been killed, I'd have graduated next month." Sadness coated her voice. So much lost at the time, yet now she was on the road to recovering her life and adding to it. She no longer wanted the life she once had. Robin wanted the life she was being offered now—Adam, the clan, the job, all of it. If she could come up with the money for the tuition, she could attend her last semester online and have her degree in a few months.

"You should finish your degree. You have so much to offer people," Tabitha said.

The bathroom door creaked open and Harmony stepped out wearing jeans and a sweatshirt. Her hair was pulled back in a ponytail, revealing a haunted look in her eyes. She limped on her mangled leg.

"If you're calm enough, I'll have Bethany heal your leg." Raja pulled out his cell to call his mate.

"I mean your people no harm, and I do appreciate you taking me in. I'm sorry I've been…uneasy." Harmony sank onto the chair, releasing a sigh.

Raja put the phone to his ear. "Love, have Shadow bring you over.

Harmony has shifted and we need you to heal her."

Tabitha leaned forward, resting her arms on her thighs. "Harmony, beside Henry, are you running from anyone else? We need to know, not only for your safety, but for my clan as well, so please be truthful."

"Just the clan in Ohio. I couldn't return and I was scared another clan would force me to return. It was a miracle I escaped. I'd rather be alone than to go through the violence again." Harmony's gaze fell to the floor.

Robin could feel the torment surging from Harmony.

"We won't send you to Ohio. The situation there will need to be dealt with. They can't continue to discard the unworthy to Henry." Tabitha looked to Raja who put away his cell.

"Tabitha is right," he said. "Once we've dealt with another situation on our plate, we will contact the Alpha of the Ohio Tigers."

"They will see me dead for violating their trust." Harmony cried.

"We won't let that happen," Tabitha tried to reassure her. "You're safe here."

"First we need to care for your leg. Bethany's on her way. Felix will need to come in to hold you while she's healing your leg. Could I take a look at it now?" Once Harmony nodded Raja strolled toward her.

"I'm not going to attack anyone." Harmony pulled the leg of her jeans up, allowing him to see the wound on her leg.

"It's mainly for precaution." He knelt in front of her, examining the damage. "Healing of a wound this extensive is extremely painful. It will help Bethany if you're completely still while she's working on your leg. Robin will help me hold your arms while Felix will keep your leg straight."

"Me?" Robin raised an eyebrow.

"Harmony connected with you, so your presence might keep her calm. Others have been trying to get her to shift for days with no results. She seems to trust you." Raja smiled.

Harmony appeared much younger than twenty. "I won't be any trouble," she said.

"I know you won't." Robin scooted forward on the sofa to lay her hand over Harmony's. "Don't worry, it will be fine. I'll be by your side. Healing will take a lot from you so I'll doubt you'll be up to talking. How about I come over after breakfast and we can talk then?"

"I don't want to talk about it." Harmony flinched under Raja's touch on her leg.

"We're going to need information about what happened to prevent further suffering." Raja moved her leg to view the other side. "This is a nasty wound. Even after Bethany heals it, you're going to have some internal healing. You're going to need to take it easy for a bit. That means staying here."

"Fine, but does the guard have to be at the door? I feel like a prisoner."

"For the next few days, yes. It's possible your leg could turn septic. A guard outside will be able to smell if your condition worsens and can alert Bethany or Doc." Tabitha looked around the apartment. "Your meals will be delivered, and unlike the last few days you need to eat. You're malnourished and your wound won't heal completely until you start taking care of your body."

Shadow opened the door, peaking inside before allowing Bethany to enter. "It's nice to see you've shifted. I've been waiting to heal your wound." She walked toward Harmony.

Raja straightened from his kneeling position, laying his hand on Bethany's shoulder to stop her. "Shadow, please ask Felix to come in."

Bethany leaned to her mate, keeping her voice a whisper. "Is that wise?"

"Harmony knows and it's fine. Right, Harmony?" Raja turned to the injured tigress.

Harmony nodded. "Yes, sir…" The rest of her words died on her tongue.

The tension surging through Harmony's body flowed through Robin's until she thought she was drowning in terror. She'd pull her hand away if the young tigress didn't have a death grip on it. She placed her other hand on top, rubbing her thumb over Harmony's knuckles. "Adam mentioned I'd feel some of the emotions from the clan members, especially when touching, because of his connection to you and his level within the clan. Harmony has no connection to the Alaskan Tigers, so why do I feel it with her?" Robin asked Raja.

"You should only feel a prickle, but now that you mention the sensation, I have it as well." Raja frowned. "Tabitha?"

Tabitha nodded. "I sense it too. I'm so use to feeling everyone's emotions that I didn't pay attention. Harmony has no connections to our clan." She shook her head. "It doesn't make sense."

Raja glanced at Shadow, and then at Felix. They each nodded. He ran his hand through his hair and took a deep breath. "She hasn't found her mate yet, so that's not it."

"Could it be through Henry?" Tabitha looked to Felix. "Technically he's connected by being his twin. That's why twin shifters are rarely in different clans. Their emotions are tied together and to have them dedicated to two different Alphas would cause conflicting feelings in each of them."

"It's possible I guess. Henry gave no oath to the Ohio Tigers. They don't consider him one of us because of his condition." Felix's hands balled into fists. "He's only there because their doctor works with mentally ill patients. If Henry bit Harmony, she'd have a connection to me. Body fluids would bring the bond to life."

"Shit!" Tabitha sank back on the sofa. "Harmony, did Henry?"

Tears fell down Harmony's face. She shook her head. "I'm sorry, I shouldn't be here."

113

"Shhh." Bethany wrapped her arm around Harmony. "None of this is your fault."

"I cause problems everywhere I go," she mumbled.

"No you don't, however this will affect your life, more so if you choose to relocate to another clan. You will still have a connection to us through Felix, no matter where you go." Raja dropped his hand to his side. "We can't change this. We need to focus on healing your leg. The bed would be a better spot to do it. Bethany, you ready?"

Bethany nodded. "If Harmony is."

Bethany and Raja helped Harmony to the bed. They situated the pillows behind her and Raja placed his hands on her shoulders. Robin took Harmony's hands in hers. Tabitha sat at the end of the bed.

"Whatever you do don't shift," Bethany said, and then ordered Shadow and Felix to stand close. "Felix is going to hold your legs. Your connection with him might become stronger, so we need to make sure you don't move while I'm healing you. He'll make sure he only touches you over your jeans to keep the connection minimal, not skin to skin contact. Now just relax."

Felix wrapped his hands around Harmony's ankles. Robin felt a sensation of emotions soar. She met Harmony's gaze and smiled. "You can do this."

Bethany nodded. "Everyone ready?" Without waiting for an answer, she placed her hands on the wound. The moment a glowing light shone from her hands, Harmony's body convulsed on the bed, fighting them.

"It's okay, Harmony, we're almost done. Just hang in there. Don't shift on us. You're doing great, sweetie," Robin urged. She clenched her teeth as Harmony's pain escalated through her.

Robin's link to Adam sprang to life. *Love! What's going on?* She heard his voice in her mind, His presence, though distant, helped her relax. She wasn't sure how he did it, maybe it was another benefit of mating, either way she

114

was grateful.

She divided her concentration for a moment, just long enough to let Adam know what happened. *I'm fine. Thank you. We've made progress with Harmony. Bethany is healing her now.*

You're an amazing woman, Robin Zimmer. He stayed with her, easing the pain she sensed through Harmony until it died away. Robin was left exhausted. Her body ached in too many places. It was as if she went through the healing with Harmony. She didn't miss the flood of emotions and pain, only the comfort of Adam. *He'll be home soon.*

Home? When did she begin to accept the Alaska Tigers compound as her home?

Chapter Fourteen

Adam slumped in his seat. He had less than an hour to regain the strength he used comforting Robin from so many miles away. He let out a deep breath, releasing the tension he took from Robin. The fear that had coursed through her woke him from a deep sleep, nearly half a continent away. Now with the knowledge she was safe, he forced his muscles to relax.

"You felt it as well?" Ty asked, frowning.

He nodded. "Through Robin, but I don't understand why. Harmony isn't from our clan." Adam kept his voice low to avoid waking the others.

"Henry's body fluids connected her to Felix and in turn us. We'll have to do something about this after we get back. Henry might be beyond help due to this unspeakable action from the Ohio Alpha." Ty's head rested against the back of the chair, his eyes closed.

"It will be tough on Felix. He knows our ways, he'll understand. We should explore all options before settling on action. Killing Henry may be our only choice to keep others safe."

"Understanding and accepting are different. You and Felix are Tabitha's best guards, losing either of you will jeopardize her safety. Not to mention we're family. I don't want to see any of our family hurting." Ty pushed his chair back, reclining again. "Get some more rest, we'll be there soon. We'll deal with the Ohio and Texas clans when this shit with Pierce is over."

Dealing with them meant taking the unit's Alpha out of power. Which meant either utter chaos, fighting amongst themselves to elect a new Alpha, or the clans were so used to being controlled they would be relieved for a calmer existence. Shifters with emotional issues were more difficult to deal with.

Adam knew through their connection, Robin had agreed to help anyone who wanted to work through their issues, but she was only one person. They couldn't bring in outside councilors to help with shifter problems without exposing themselves. Too much risk unless they wanted to expose themselves. Would the obstacles never end? Would the Alaskan Tigers never have time to just sit back and enjoy their lives, or would there always be something jeopardizing their safety?

"Ty." He waited until his Alpha opened his eyes. "Maybe we should create a specialized team for clan safety. Danger could get more precarious in the coming months, especially taking down two clan Alphas. Some might see us as a threat. It might be wise for Tabitha to come out to all clans as Queen of the Tigers. Something to think about."

"Good point, we'll consult the book and Tabitha when we get back to Alaska." Ty's eyes closed again letting Adam know their conversation was over for now.

One disaster at a time and they'd survive. They also had to consider who was more of a threat, Ohio or Texas? Who would be their next mission?

Robin sank to the floor utterly exhausted, resting her head against the side of the bed. No one other than herself and Bethany seemed to be suffering, which added to her confusion.

Raja knelt in front of her, taking her hand in his. "Just rest, Robin. Some of it will pass shortly. You'll still feel tired. It won't be so bad."

Her rolling stomach and pounding head eased with Raja's touch. "Why does your touch help? I thought only Adam's would."

"As the Lieutenant my touch will help any member of our clan, as long as they are committed to us. Ty and Tabitha's abilities work the same way. Bethany's skill is slightly different since she's a healer. She carries the gene to shift without shifting.

"That means you consider yourself part of our family now." Tabitha squatted down next to them, wrapping her arms around Robin's neck. "Welcome to the family."

A smile pulled her lips, and tears threatened to fall. She was a part of such a close-knit family. "I guess I have."

They stayed cuddled on the floor waiting for the affects to past until Harmony's whispered voice called to Robin.

"It's okay, I'm right here." Robin took Harmony's hand. Glancing up, she found Harmony curled into a tight ball in the center of the bed.

"Why did it hurt you more than anyone else?"

Tabitha stood and moved to the edge of the bed. "I believe it's because you've formed a connection with Robin. She's the only one you feel any loyalty to. The rest of us felt your pain through her. In a way, Robin served to dull the pain. Normally the Elders do that for the clan, which is why for serious healing one of the Elders is normally there to act as a buffer."

That explained why Robin was feeling Harmony's emotions nearly as strong as she felt Adam's. "Will it wear off?" Robin asked.

"If Harmony commits herself to the Alaskan Tigers, you'll feel the connection just as Ty and I do. If she commits to another clan it could be worse because her commitments would be divided." Raja helped Robin off the floor to sit on the edge of the bed next to Harmony.

"I'm sorry, I didn't mean to hurt you." Harmony forced a weak smile at Robin.

"It's all right, Harmony. There's no harm done. Everything is going to be fine. Right now you need to get some sleep." Robin wasn't sure if she was fighting just exhaustion or if Harmony's fatigue was added into the mix. Either way she needed to get some rest. She wanted to be awake when the team went after Pierce. She needed to be connected to Adam to know he was okay. If she was asleep, she might not know if something serious happened to him, so Robin wasn't taking the chance.

"Stay with me until I'm asleep, please." Harmony rested back on the bed, her eyelids half closed.

"Okay." Robin ran her hand through Harmony's thick red hair, moving it out of her face.

"Felix, Shadow, and Korbin, take Tabitha and Bethany home. I'll stay with Robin until she's done." Raja stepped toward Bethany, wrapping his arm around her. "I'll be along shortly, get some rest." He pressed his lips to hers.

Watching the intimacy between Raja and Bethany made Robin long to have the same with Adam—to have him by her side. With his support she felt like she could take on the world, instead of cowering in fear. "You don't have to stay, Raja."

"If the emotions become too much for you again, I'm the only one who can help you." He leaned against the wall next to the bed watching everyone file out. "Lance has taken his post outside."

Robin rubbed her hand over Harmony's shoulder. Silence engulfed the room. Emotions still played through her, most of them Harmony's, but at least they weren't as draining as before. Minutes passed before the young tigress drifted to sleep. "Can she feel my emotions as well?" Robin asked Raja.

He gazed down at her and shook her head. "Not now, she's going through too much of her own turmoil to feel anything else. It's doubtful it will be different in the future since the connection was built out of her devotion and loyalty to you. Unless Ty and I are gravely injured, only our mates will feel our emotions through the connection. If we were to force

120

them upon others they can be felt to a degree. Think of a box filled with rocks. The heavier it is, the better chance of someone besides our mate would feel it."

"She owes me nothing." She looked down at Harmony, lying in a curled ball. She was so young and innocent.

"That's not how Harmony sees it. There was a link between you as if you were the Alpha Female here. Even if she commits to the clan, if at any time your beliefs don't line up with the Elders, Harmony will follow you over us. Do you understand what that means?"

Robin had an idea, but didn't want to say what she was thinking. "Not completely."

"Hypnotically, if you gain more bonds while helping the injured, you could create your own following. A clan and Alpha Female without being a shifter." His eyes seemed to search her for a reaction. "It's something that's never happened. You could be the first."

"I have no desire to do that, nor the means. I didn't mean to poach your territory or position." Would her connection to Harmony made things difficult for Adam?

"You have the means with Adam. He's strong enough to lead his own clan, only his commitment to Ty keeps him here, holding him back. If anyone were to convince him to step out on his own, it could be his mate." Raja straightened, not moving away from the wall. "With your abilities you would be in the same position as Tabitha. The connection would take the place of shifting."

"That isn't going to happen. I feel Adam's bond to the clan and nothing could distort that. I fell in love with the man he is now. Changing something as big as his commitment to his clan—his family—would change the man I love. I'd do nothing to jeopardize that." She moved her hand from Harmony and rose, meeting Raja's gaze head on. "Adam's bond to the clan has become my connection. When I arrived here I said some things, especially to Bethany, that were rude. I was hurting and wanted to spoil everyone else's happiness. Now I see what your clan truly is. My commitment is to you and the clan, just as Adam's is. Don't discount that or me because I'm merely human."

A smile spread over Raja's face. "We need fighters like you in the clan. Welcome to the family, Robin. It's an honor to have you among us."

She took a moment to think about his words and realized the fight she lost running across the country had returned. She was willing to fight for Adam's honor, and for Harmony's safety. Robin couldn't stand up against a shifter's speed or strength, but she had her own assets to contribute to the clan.

"It's a privilege to be part of such a family. I never thought I'd want a life like this, now I realize I've been searching for a true home, and Adam, all my life." She paused. "Most humans believe in soul mates. I never did until now. Adam is my soul mate."

Moonlight cascaded through the room, giving Robin enough light to see Raja standing next to her. His hand gently shook her arm. "Robin, are you awake?"

She rolled, checking the bedside clock. Damn it, she wanted to be up when the team landed. "What is it? Is it Adam?"

"No, it's not them. They've arrived at the site, and the Kodiak Bears landed fifteen minutes ago. They're still on the landing strip. They're putting together a plan of attack before setting out again. It's Harmony. She woke up and is having a breakdown. I hated to wake you but she needs you. She won't tell anyone else what's going on."

Robin sat up in bed, making sure her nightshirt was covering her body. "Okay, give me a minute to get dressed."

"I'll wait in the living room for you and then I'll take you to her." He stepped away from the bed and left the room.

She pulled on her jeans and grabbed a sweater from her bag, tugging it over her head. As she dressed, she forgot her worries of what Adam would be doing soon. Only Harmony's fear pushed her quicker, not giving her a moment to think of anything else. She slid her feet into her sneakers, cursing that she hadn't picked up something more suitable for the snow yet.

Raja was waiting for her by the door. The only light came from a small lamp by the sofa. "Bethany's still sleeping. Do you have enough light to see?"

"I'm fine." She ran her fingers through her hair, trying to pull herself together. "Let's go."

Raja nodded and opened the door. "Thomas was on guard duty. He said one minute everything was fine and then Harmony woke up screaming. He went to her to figure out what was wrong. She just kept screaming your name."

Raja kept pace with Robin as they jogged toward Harmony's apartment. The closer they got, Harmony's screams sliced through the air, forcing Robin to run faster. There was something heartbreaking about the cries.

Thomas opened the door, allowing her to skid right past him and straight to Harmony. "Harmony, what is it?"

She went to take Harmony's hand until Raja placed his hand on her shoulder. "Careful. When a shifter is angry they can snap at the first sight of someone. We can't have you getting hurt."

"Henry…oh God, Henry…he's coming," Harmony cried, her fingers balling the blanket. "You've got to do something. He's coming for me!"

Ignoring Raja's warning, Robin sank onto the bed, wrapping her arms around Harmony. "Shhh, sweetie, you're safe here."

"Get Felix here immediately," Raja ordered Thomas who was still in the doorway.

Robin glanced over the top of Harmony's head at Raja. "Is that wise?"

"As his twin, Felix might be able to feel Henry. He'll at least know if Henry makes it to Alaska." Raja sat on the edge of the bed. "Harmony, how do you know this? Any details you can give us might help us stop him before he even gets to Alaska."

"I just know. I can't explain it. I only know he's coming. He knows I'm here." She curled into Robin like a small child cuddling against their mother after a nightmare.

Soothing her, Robin looked to Raja. "How is this possible? How does he even know where she is? Is it through the connection? I thought he was sedated, that the Ohio Tigers had him under control."

"Since he's never shifted, the bond to Felix is more one way. Felix can feel Henry, but not the other way around. It could be through Harmony's connection to him."

Felix ran in the room, gun in his hand. "What's wrong?"

"Harmony believes Henry is on his way here. Can you confirm that?" Raja asked.

"I don't know. I've never been very in tune with my brother. I can try." Felix's eyes drifted shut, and he breathed deep. "I can feel his excitement. He's on the move, he's not here. The surroundings are different. I can't identify where he is exactly. He's not at the clan's compound in Ohio."

"I told you he's coming," Harmony screamed, anger filling her tone.

"I believe you. We're just trying to find out how close he is," Raja spoke calmly.

"You've got to help me. He's going to kill me." Harmony's body shook with fear.

"You're safe here, Harmony. Nothing is going to happen to you." Raja glanced back at Felix. "Who's guarding Tabitha?"

"Korbin is with her, and Thomas stayed with her until Jayden or Drew got there. I alerted them when Thomas called me." Felix slid his gun back into his holster.

"Very good." Raja pushed the button on his earpiece to communicate with the other guards. "Korbin, take Tabitha to my quarters with Bethany. I want the women together until further notice."

"Do you want me to go back to Tabitha? Or stay?" Felix seemed unsure what to do.

"Besides Harmony, you're the only connection to Henry. We need you here for now. If we can settle Harmony, we'll take her back to my quarters as well. She can rest in Robin's room. If that's okay with you, Robin?"

"It's fine. Do you think Doc could give her something to calm her down and let her sleep?" Robin ran her hand down Harmony's back, soothing her.

Raja nodded. "If she agrees."

"When Henry comes, I need to be able to get away. Giving me something to sleep would make me easy prey for him."

"He's not going to get anywhere near you." Felix stepped around Raja and approached Harmony. "You have my word. I blocked my connection to him for my own sanity. He's dangerous. I won't let him get anywhere near you."

Robin squeezed Harmony to her. "They're twins. Felix can't help that he looks so much like Henry, but I swear Felix is a good man. He will protect you." Still feeling Harmony's doubt, she continued. "Our connection is too one sided for you to feel my trust in him. Put your trust in me that I trust him. It will be fine. I promise."

Harmony nodded and rested her head against Robin's shoulder. "Okay." Her eyes drifted shut, exhaustion filling her body.

"What now?" Robin glanced to Raja, wondering what they were going to do about the new danger. If Henry arrived before the team got back from Virginia did they have enough guards to protect everyone?

"We wait. Until we know where Henry is, there's nothing we can do. When Felix recognizes his brother's location, we'll act on it immediately. If he comes to Alaska, we'll stop him before he gets to the compound. Hopefully the morning light will bring more information. By morning one of our problems will no longer be an issue. We can then focus on Henry and Ohio." Raja hit his earpiece. "Go ahead."

"Until then, keeping everyone together with our resources surrounding the area will be the best protection," Felix explained. "We'll hunker down in Raja's quarters for now, and in the morning we'll have a plan of action. It would be good if Harmony was able to rest. Her anxiety will only encourage Henry further."

"Harmony, would you take something to rest while Felix, the other guards, and I watch over you?" Robin nudged a pillow under Harmony's back.

Harmony nodded, her body growing heavier as sleep pressed down on her.

Raja turned away from the window, coming back to stand next to the bed. "I'll have Doc meet us at my quarters. Harmony looks exhausted. We don't want her falling asleep until we get her to your room."

His cell phone rang. A lump caught in Robin's throat. At this time of the night she feared it would have something to do with the team in Virginia. She could sense Adam, he was safe, but that's all she could tell. There was too much interference with Harmony's emotions especially with her arms around the girl.

Raja unclipped his cell phone and checked the caller id. "Felix, take the women to my quarters I need to take this."

Robin wanted to wait to know what was happening, but she couldn't leave Harmony, especially not alone with the man she feared because of his similarity to his brother. She'd have to wait until Raja returned to his quarters.

Chapter Fifteen

Twenty minutes later, Robin collapsed in the living room chair. Harmony was finally asleep. Robin could have passed out on the bed beside the young girl. There was just too much going on. She needed to be awake. Adam's anxiousness was teasing her exhaustion. Without a doubt, she knew the team was on their way to Pierce.

Raja stepped through the door, glancing around the room. Tabitha and Felix were on one sofa, while Bethany lounged on the other. Shadow sat nearby, Jayden and Drew guarded the door, while Thomas and Korbin kept a watchful-eye outside. "The team is moving in and they'll call when it's over."

"There's something more. What's going on?" Bethany pulled her legs under her body, giving her mate room to sit.

He glanced toward the guest room. "Is Harmony asleep?" When Robin nodded, Raja continued. "Jinx's clan picked up a phone call to Pierce only minutes ago. It seems that the Ohio Alpha has been working with Pierce for some time. Pierce has been holding something over the Ohio Alpha's head to get him to do his bidding. I don't know if it ties into what happened with Henry and Harmony. It's too big of a coincidence to overlook."

"So what's the plan with the Ohio Tigers? We can't continue to let things go as they are." Bethany snuggled into Raja.

"Actually Ty wants Tabitha to consult the book. Adam suggested it would be a perfect time for you to come out as the Queen of the Tigers, and Ty seems to agree." Raja ran his hand through his hair. "It makes sense, and will give us a chance to start bringing the clans together under one rule."

Tabitha nodded. "Okay, I'll do that. What about now?"

"Depending on what the book says, or what you want to do, there's talk some of the guards will go to Ohio after they finish with Pierce. You have to consult the book before they're done. Ty wants to know our decision when he calls." Raja rested his head against Bethany's shoulder. "Felix will stay here with Robin and Harmony, while you and I check the book."

"Adam mentioned Tabitha is the Queen of Tigers, but how will it work?" Robin could barely focus with her nerves and exhaustion on edge, but she was interested in learning how things were going to change for shifters. "Right now each clan has its own ruler. With them spread out all over the country, how are you going to rule everyone?"

Tabitha twisted in her seat to look at Robin. "Each clan will still have an Alpha, but there will be another level of authority—Ty and myself. Each Alpha and Lieutenant will report to us. No clan will be able to rule their own way any longer because that's how we end up with Alphas in Ohio and Texas abusing their followers. That will end, even if I have to take every Alpha out of power myself. What happened to Tex and Harmony can't continue."

"Tabitha will unite all tiger shifters," Raja said. "She will also help to bring other shifters together. The Kodiak Bears have joined us in our fight thanks to Ty helping them when we came to Alaska, soon other shifters will join us as well. Shifters will unite in time. First we must unite the tigers." Raja closed his eyes as he cuddled Bethany against him.

Robin knew nothing would be done until the morning light. Would the team take down Pierce so they could focus on the next obstacle? Or would Pierce once again slip through their grasp?

Anxiety teased along the edge of Adam's nerves. He wanted to get the mission over and go back to his mate. They were nearing the house where Pierce was. All the years of hunting Pierce would finally pay off. He would never be a threat again, but for some reason Adam had a feeling this would not end the issue with the rogues. Someone else would step into Pierce's position until they could take all the rogues down.

"We'll take them down." Ty glanced over at Adam. "You know how this works, so don't look at me like that. I can feel your apprehension. We're thinking the same thing. With Victor and Pierce out of the equation it will be easier to take the rogues out. They will either fight among themselves or separate. There's only so much we can do at one time. Right now we need to focus on Pierce."

Adam turned his gaze to the road, before looking to the back of the SUV. Styx sat in the backseat with Marcus, and Taber, who sat in the seat furthest away, was trying to catch a few quick winks before the fight began. "We'll keep our clan safe," Adam said. "It's priority. Everything else will fall into place."

Ty leaned closer, whispering to not wake Taber. "Robin is part of the clan now, and from what I hear, she's been a major help with Harmony. It's highly unusual for a human to have that connection. She'll have to learn how to work out a balance of two sets of emotions. Once Harmony's been mated hopefully it will calm Robin's link to her, until then, Robin might have a rough time. Harmony's been through a lot and the dam holding her emotions could break, spewing a lot of shit forward. Raja and I won't be able to help like we would with another clan member, since Harmony isn't connected to us. She feels loyalty only to Robin."

"I'll do what I can to help Robin. My touch should ease Harmony's effect on her." Adam steered the SUV down the deserted road, toward the outskirts of town. "What are you planning if Harmony isn't willing to make the commitment to the Alaskan Tigers? Will you allow her to stay at the compound if she's only committed to Robin?"

"I won't ask her to leave as long as she doesn't cause any problems. If Harmony doesn't join us we will have to rely on Robin to know that Harmony is not betraying us. However, if she does join us, if Robin is ever opposed to what's in the clans best interest, Harmony will create conflicting emotions. Robin has reassured Raja that she's with our clan, and you, but her discomfort is something we need to consider." Ty stared out of the window.

Adam raised an eyebrow. "Reassured Raja? When did that happen?"

"Your mate is working her way into our clan. She and Raja are becoming quite a pair. Raja's been helping ease Harmony's emotions from Robin, giving Robin a chance to get used to them without feeling overwhelmed. His touch will help in short bursts so he's only assisting when it's overpowering."

Adam couldn't hide the smile from his face. His mate was finding her own way in his clan without him there to guide her. The mission might have been just what she needed to overcome her apprehension. If she didn't become a part of the clan, then he would have been split between his clan and his mate. Dividing himself and his attention between the two would be difficult, but if she had her own purpose, then they'd combine together, creating a solid and lasting bond.

"If you've ever thought of starting your own clan, you've always been strong enough to do so, and with Robin's connection with Harmony it would make you stronger, especially if she can continue to make those connections." Ty added as Adam stopped the SUV at the meeting spot, less than a mile from Pierce. This was their gathering point with the Kodiak Bears, who were following in the second vehicle.

Shoving the SUV into Park, Adam turned to his Alpha. Did Ty think he would leave even after all they've been through? "I have no desire to leave the Alaskan Tigers. It's my home, you're my family."

Ty nodded and opened his door. Pushing open his own door, Adam followed Ty's lead, and checked the weapons and gear.

He wanted to reach Robin, to tell her how he felt about her, but if this attack went bad she didn't need that to be her final thought. He wanted her to remember their time together, her first night with a tiger.

Robin paced the room suddenly feeling caged in. Six months ago, she had a perfectly normal life, besides her marriage. Now, every turn she made she was surrounded by danger. Would the threats to her new home and family ever pass, or would this be her life now?

"It's not always like this." Felix stood near the window, looking out to the darkness of the night.

She had tried occupying her time with watching the comings and goings outside. Every once in awhile someone would pass by one of the lights from a cabin, or around the perimeter, giving her something to focus on. Other than that it was just darkness as far as the eye could see. She suspected Felix could see further and better or why else would he continue to stare into the night.

"Danger has surrounded us since Ty found Tabitha, and rejuvenated with Pierce, but there was a time it was safe to be a shifter. No one knew about shifters, unless you were one of us. We didn't have to worry about people attacking our homes, or compound. The occasional rogue was the only real threat." Felix turned from the window to face her. "It will be like that again, the book has promised that. We have to solider through this fight and we will have safety in the near future. This clan is the type of world I want for my children, so I'm willing to fight for it."

She leaned against the armrest of the sofa, watching Felix. Tabitha and Bethany had gone in the other room to get a little more sleep, leaving her alone with Felix, the guards still at the door. "With all the threats I'm just wondering if I'm more of a hindrance as a human instead of truly helping."

"When there's time I'll take you to the gym, if you'd like. You'll see the changes there better than anywhere. Being mated to a shifter, even though you're human, you will age slower. You'll see changes in your speed and strength. It's not as considerable as shifters, but it's still remarkable."

She gazed past him to the window, thinking about what he said. "If the compound was compromised could I hold my own if something happened?"

"I suspect with a little training you could until help arrived. It's hard for mates to work together in training, especially in your case. Adam would be easier on you, unwilling to push you because he wants to protect you. If you want to learn, I'll work with you." He slid his hand into the pocket of his jeans. "We don't know how long the danger will last before the clan is once again safe, so the more people who can protect themselves, the better. We have guards patrolling the compound at all hours. If you travel outside the compound it's better to know how to shoot a gun to protect yourself. Knowledge of hand-to-hand combat would be helpful as well."

She could shoot, maybe not as well as she would like, but she hadn't shot a gun since she was a child. Robin didn't have any skills in hand-to-hand combat. If someone attacked her she had very little chance of defending herself adequately. "I would appreciate that."

Chapter Sixteen

The moon was full, forcing Adam and the others to the shadows of the trees in case Pierce looked out his window. Adam and Ty moved together, almost as one, getting to the spot where they could view the house while the second team got into place. The Kodiak Bears divided through both teams, giving them added strength.

Adam's heart raced, beating frantically against his chest. He clenched his gun in its holster. No one planned to shift unless the situation got out of hand. The goal was to get in and out within twenty minutes. While Adam's team searched for Pierce, the other teams would divide and conquer. Jinx, with the assistance of Turi and Trey, would search for the hidden room, while Marcus and the other guards would search the house for any information that might help find the other rogues.

"Don't get eager, this is my kill if possible. I will gain justice for my mate, for Bethany, and everyone else who has been effected by Pierce." Ty slid his gun from his holster.

"We'll honor that if we can, but your safety is more important than who gets the kill. I promised Tabitha I would bring you back without a scratch." Adam pulled his gun from his hip holster, and clicked the safety. "Let's do this."

Scurrying through the shadows, they made their way to the front of the house. Adam stayed in front of Ty. If a trap waited for them inside, Adam wanted to make sure his Alpha wasn't in the direct line of fire. Styx squeezed in beside him, working his talent on the lock and within seconds it popped open. The fact Styx knew how to pick a lock surprised no one, after all Styx had been an assassin at one time, working for a former Alpha as his personal executioner.

Easing into the entryway, Adam spotted a tripwire. The fail-safe would alert Pierce if anyone made it past the door. Adam signaled the others, and then carefully stepped over it as he went right and Styx went left. With a clean sweep of the living quarters, Adam and Styx headed for the stairs. Taber aimed his gun at the overhead railing, guarding the team as the rest made their way up the steps.

Scanning the hall with his eyes and gun, Adam took in a deep breath. He tried to sense which room Pierce was in, and if there were any other human or shifter scents coming from the other rooms. He waited for Taber to join them before stepping aside so everyone was in a tight group. "Pierce is at the end of the hall, asleep." His whispered tone could only be heard by those next to him. "This feels too easy. We been after him too long, it should be a harder fight."

"Maybe he's tired of the fight?" The group of men looked at Styx, who shrugged his shoulders. "I spent longer than I care to remember as an assassin. You eventually tire of the chase. It should never be routine to kill someone. Sociopaths do it for the sport, but the rest of us do it to keep innocents safe."

"Or it could be a trap," Taber pointed out.

"I don't smell any explosives, or other shifters around us." Adam's pulse beat frantically on the side of his neck. "If it's a trap, it's just Pierce. We've got enough man power to take him down even with a fight."

"We're doing this. Let's go," Ty ordered.

"Stay behind us," Adam whispered, moving down the hall with Styx at his side. Ty was next and Taber brought up the rear watching their ass.

Since arriving, Adam felt a connection to Robin, almost as if she was standing next to him, guiding him. They were as one when her voice called to him. *Be safe.* He would be, and if all went well, in a matter of hours he'd be in her arms again.

Adam pushed the door open, resting his finger just above the trigger of his gun. He scanned the room and ended at the bed. Adam took a step back. The horrific smell surrounding the room caught in his throat, making it hard to breathe. A clearly poisoned Pierce lay in the middle of the bed, his limbs stretched out and tied to the bedpost corners.

"What the hell?" Styx blinked from the stench.

Adam held his breath in the sickening air. He stepped forward, noticing a piece of paper. Pierce was still alive. There was no telling how long before the poison would kill him. If Ty wanted the kill, he'd have to do it soon. Either way this lacked the real fight that Adam and the rest of the team were looking forward to.

Adam snatched the paper from Pierce's chest. He read the note.

Pierce has been growing more and more desperate to kill your clan. His insanity has begun to jeopardize Bratva and I will not stand for that. Instead, I offer him to you on a golden platter with the knowledge that if you come after us we will be forced to kill you. To eliminate your problem further, I've taken care of Pierce's rogues that were no use to me and Bratva. Enjoy your kill. Keith, US Bratva leader.

Adam had hoped Bratva wouldn't be an issue after they had killed Victor. Obviously someone else had stepped in to lead the Bratva. They would have to completely dispend that organization if they were going to protect their kind.

Ty stepped up beside him, with Styx close by. Adam handed the note to Ty. Ty might be their Alpha and have to prove he was able to take care of himself and the clan, but there was a reason Elders had guards and it wasn't because they were weak. In a direct challenge a guard could do nothing to help the Alpha, but when it came to rogues they would protect their Alpha to the death. Whatever they were going to do, they needed to get it done quickly because the smell of the room was getting stronger by the minute.

Pierce moaned and struggled against the chains, his eyes still closed. His movement sent new waves of pigment odor through the room.

"Whatever you're going to do needs to be done now." Adam stepped to the side, giving Ty direct access to Pierce.

"I wanted him to put up a fight, to beg for his life. At the very least the bastard will know what's coming." Ty looked down at the gun in his hand. "Pierce took the life of my mate's family, which left her an orphan, and I had to watch him kill Bethany's parents and sister. I'm doing this for all the lives he destroyed in his wake. He will know I'm the one who took his life. I only wish I was less civilized, that I could torture him as he had done to Bethany and countless others."

Adam wanted to torture the bastard too for the hell he put Robin through, but the Alaskan clan were better than that. They wouldn't stoop to Pierce's level. It's not who they were. His fingers began to tighten around the gun until he was afraid he might break the handle. He forced his shoulders to relax.

Pierce's eyes opened, fear made them glow, bringing his weretiger close to the surface. As a bitten were he wouldn't be able to shift without a full moon, therefore he couldn't heal himself or break free from the chains.

"How did you get in here?" Pain filled Pierce's voice.

Ty stepped next to the bed, keeping his gun aimed on Pierce. "Where can I find Keith?"

"I don't know." Pierce's eyes closed and his face clenched in pain.

"Open your eyes, damn it. Do you know why I'm here?"

Pierce opened his eyes, just barely. He pulled against the chains again. "To kill me."

"Damn right. You killed the families of people I care for. You tortured and killed more people than I care to remember while we were chasing you. Now it all ends. Do you have anything to say?"

"Killing me won't end the threat. If it's not me, it will be someone else. Keith is a cold blood murderer. He'll find Tabitha and kill her. It won't be as quick as I would have done. Her death will be on your hands." He took a deep a breath. "If you expect me to beg for my life it won't happen. This poison will kill me before long, so either way I'm dead."

"Begging would have done no good," Ty said.

Adam stood next to Ty, his gun pointed at Pierce. Styx mirrored Adam's stance at the end of the bed. Ty holstered his gun and took out a syringe from his pocket. Before they had left Alaska, Doc had mixed up a deadly batch of drugs that would kill even the strongest shifter. It was humane and would appear as if Pierce had a heart attack.

"Tell me what you had on the Ohio Tigers to get them to do your business?" Ty twisted the cap off the syringe.

"You haven't figured it out yet?" Pierce laughed, yet in too much pain to be heartfelt. "Keith was the Ohio Alpha, he abandoned his clan to lead a stronger group, Bravta."

Adam was thankful for the connection he still kept active with Robin. He wasn't sure if Ty had a link to Tabitha opened, so Adam passed the information to his mate. *Get this news to Raja and Tabitha. Ohio's Alpha was Keith and he's leading the U.S. Bravta. No other information yet. Get Connor on it.*

"You'll go to your grave knowing we found you because Robin Zimmer came to us." Ty told Pierce. "You screwed up messing with her. She's got fight and helped bring you down."

Pierce once again struggled against the chains. "If Keith has no interest in Robin, know that Randolph has been my second for years and he will pick up where I left off. Your problems are not over. Randolph will revenge my name and see your clan dead."

"I'll take them all down. My clan is my family, mess with one of us you are messing with all of us. Your rogues are no match for us." Ty shoved the needle into Pierce's arm and pushed down the plunger.

Watching him squirm as the drugs hit his system seemed unsatisfying. For years they had sought Pierce, always finding the lead a little too late and being a few steps behind him. Tonight Pierce's life would finally end, but Adam was spoiling for a good fight, to put all those hours he had spent in the gym to work. His tiger paced within him. This was just a disappointment to both of them.

Adam watched as the stare of death took over Pierce's eyes.

"Is everything all right up there? It's eerie quiet." Jinx's voice sprang live through Adam's earpiece.

"Subject had been terminated. How is the situation on your end?" Adam asked.

"We've found something. It might be the room."

Adam looked at Ty for instructions before making a move.

Ty raised his hand to his eyepiece. "Marcus, when you're done search the upstairs rooms. We're going to join Jinx." Ty moved to the door, and everyone fell in place. "Jinx, we're on our way, wait for us."

Chapter Seventeen

After Robin passed the information about Keith to Raja and Tabitha, everyone's exhaustion seemed to slip away. Now they had a purpose, they weren't just sitting around waiting for the other tiger paw to drop. Connor and Lukas were in the make-shift computer center down the hall with everything they needed to find on Keith.

Now that the Ohio Tigers no longer had an Alpha, with no leadership it could be disastrous for all involved. If that clan wasn't careful they could expose all shifters. They were abused shifters which left their actions in question. Without leadership it wasn't surprising that Henry escaped.

"What are we going to do about Ohio's Tigers?" Tabitha brought a tray full of coffee and cookies in the living room.

"We're going to send someone who can take control of the clan." Raja took a mug from the tray and sat next to Bethany on the sofa.

"Who?" Robin asked.

"The first few that spring to mind are Adam, Felix, Shadow, and Styx. Unfortunately, those who qualified don't want to leave the clan. They are content with their positions here as Elder guards. It would also make us weaker to send any of them away when Tabitha will be announcing she is Queen of the Tigers." Raja took a sip of his coffee.

"So you've decided to announce your status?" Robin grabbed a cup of coffee and looked to Tabitha.

"Not yet. The book said the time is nearing, but not until Ty is home." Tabitha pulled her legs under her. "It will be before we have to deal with the

Texas Tigers.

"If they aren't willing, then we still have a problem," Bethany said.

"They're not the only ones qualified just the most suited for it. Getting the Ohio Tigers under control before all hell breaks loose is going to be a big job." Raja checked the computer print-out on the table. "The Ohio Tigers are small, with only twelve members not including Henry or the former Alpha. It was part of the reason he didn't have a Lieutenant that could take over now. This works in our benefit. We need to temporarily combine the West Virginia and Ohio clans and have Jinx take over as their Alpha. The West Virginia Tigers can help keep Ohio in line—help them adjust to live with a normal Alpha."

"Would Jinx agree?" Tabitha set her coffee aside.

Raja shrugged his shoulders. "It's worth asking. We need him here, but right now he's our only choice. I was going to send Korbin along with Jinx, as a Lieutenant. Korbin is strong enough to take over the clan. He has little experience. This opportunity will give him a chance to prove his ability. Eventually he can take over the Ohio Tigers."

Robin leaned forward, placing her elbows on her knees and cupping her coffee in her hands. "Instead of combining the clans, why not send Jinx and Korbin, with the understanding that Korbin will take over. Jinx will only be there to consult. That way we can get Jinx back quickly and the clan will have an Alpha from the beginning."

"Robin, you should have been part of this clan years ago." Raja smiled. "I'll get in touch with Jinx and Ty to get their thoughts once they are done at the house. Tabitha, would you like to accompany me to speak with Korbin?"

"Sure." Tabitha nodded as Harmony staggered out of the bedroom.

"Harmony, you should be resting." Robin set her coffee aside and went to Harmony.

"I thought of…" Her legs wobbled and she fell to the floor.

Felix went to help Robin, but Raja held him back. "I'll get her into bed and she can tell us what she remembered." Raja walked around the sofa, bent, and scooped Harmony up in his arms in one quick motion.

Following Raja, Robin turned to Felix. "Henry's not any closer, is he?"

"No. I'm not sure where he is. He's waiting for something." Felix followed them into the bedroom.

Raja tucked Harmony into bed, pulling the blankets tight around her. "What did you remember?"

"Robin…" Harmony reached out, and when Robin's hand slipped into hers, she held it tight. "Randolph, he's a friend of Henry and the Alpha. He's not a member of the clan. He's a lone shifter. Henry will be with him."

Felix nodded. "I know Randolph. He's a weird guy, one that rubs you the wrong way. He has strange practices, and moved into the woods because he doesn't like the direction the shifters are heading. He believes that shifters are top of the food chain, therefore we could kill humans when the mood strikes."

Robin felt Harmony tense as they listened to how dangerous Randolph was. "Don't worry Harmony. I want you to just get some sleep. We're just outside if you need anything." Robin nodded for the men to follow her out. Harmony didn't need to hear any more news to make her more afraid.

After closing the door behind her, Robin turned to Raja and Felix. "How can we find Randolph if he has no connection to a clan?"

"Randolph?" Tabitha looked at them.

"He's a lone shifter that Harmony remembered having a connection to Henry. She believes if we locate Randolph we might be able to find Henry before he gets to Alaska," Felix explained.

"He's got to have something in his name, a bill, cell phone, or something. Everyone leaves a trace. I'll get Connor on it." Bethany snatched the cell phone from the end table.

Damn it, will the trouble never cease? Robin was tired of the roller coaster ride that had become her life. One minute she was thankful Adam and the team took down Pierce without any trouble, and then there was a new threat to worry about.

Adam examined the trap door while Styx and Taber stood back with Jinx and Ty in case there was a trip sensor. The twins Turi and Trey guarded nearby.

"You'd never even notice this door if you weren't feeling the wall for something," Adam said. "It blends in perfectly. From what I can tell there are no wires or anything unusual. I want everyone back in the other room while I open it. Just in case."

Ty shook his head. "You don't know what's on the other side of that door."

"That's why you need to go. I won't risk your safety." Adam pointed toward the other door. "You have to leave now so we can get out of here before that horrific smell penetrates the whole house."

"You're not doing it alone."

Adam rose from where he was squatting by the trap door. "Ty, this is my job. I was your guard before you mated and I was assigned to your mate. I can't just forget to keep you safe. Now please, we're wasting time."

"I'll stay with him. Styx, get the Alpha out of here." Taber ordered.

"Wait a second, I don't take orders, I give them. Now get out of the way." Ty stepped around Adam and tugged open the door.

It squeaked, but nothing happened. No one jumped out, and no guns or bombs exploded, just an eerie silence.

Adam shook his head at his Alpha's actions. "At least let me go in first." Adam pushed in front of his Alpha. If someone waited for them down the hall, Adam wouldn't let Ty be the first injured. It was his job and he wasn't going to let a stubborn Elder be the reason he let Ty get hurt, or the reason he had to go home and explain it to Tabitha.

"Damn guards," Ty mumbled.

"Bitch all you want, but we're here to keep you alive," Adam said. "I'm on strict orders from Tabitha to bring you back in one piece. I am not going to be the one to tell her you were hurt being the lead." Adam pointed his gun as he moved down the narrow hallway. Ty wanting to be part of the action is the reason most Elders did not go on missions with the team. They were too valuable to the clans to risk on missions.

"You two stay here, keep watch and make sure this door stays open," Taber ordered the twins.

Moving down three steps, the area turned to a concrete floor with dirt walls. It had to be an addition after the house was built. If Adam's coordinates were right, the hidden room would be under the back deck. He could smell something at the end of the narrow space. He took a deep breath, trying to distinguish the scent. A musty smell overwhelmed his senses. But deep in the space there was a tigress shifter, her fear coming down at them in waves.

"Who's there? Come out, now!" Adam called, continuing to move down the dark space.

"Wait…" Ty touched Adam's shoulder, forcing him to halt. "It's Daisy."

"Who?"

"Daisy's father left clan life a few months before we moved to Alaska. His job forced him overseas for a few years. Daisy didn't want to go. She said something bad would happen if they went. Being underage, she had no choice but to go with her father." Ty tipped his head back, taking a deep breath before opening his eyes again. "I'd know her scent anywhere. The lemony taste that it leaves in your mouth is unmistakably hers. I've never met

145

anyone with the same effect."

"I remember that." Adam nodded, unhooking his flashlight from his belt as he continued down the space. "Daisy, are you alone? We're here to help you."

The narrow hallway led to a dark open space, and in the middle of the room laid a filthy mattress. A girl huddled in the center, her arms holding her legs to her chest, with her head resting on the top.

Ty lowered his gun while Adam scanned the rest of the space with his flashlight. When Adam nodded that all was clear, Ty stepped toward the girl. "Daisy, do you remember me. It's Ty, Alpha of the Alaskan Tigers. You and your dad were part of my clan until the move." The girl's gaze followed Ty as he moved. She still remained silent.

"How long do you think she's been down here?" Adam wasn't sure how she could have survived being in this room and still have her sanity.

"Too long from the looks of it." Ty holstered his gun, holding out his hands as he stepped closer. Adam and the other guards kept their guns out, not that anyone would want to shoot in such a confined space, but they would if one of their lives depended on it.

"One hundred and twelve days." Daisy's voice was parched. Those simple words set her into a coughing fit. "He made a point of telling me every time he came down."

"Let's get you out of here and somewhere safe." Ty held a hand out to her.

She didn't move. "I'd rather you just kill me. I can't face people if they know what happened here. Nor do I want him to find me again."

"Pierce is dead, and no one outside of this room knows how we found you." Ty knelt in front of her. "Come home. Things are changing, for the better, come be part of it. You have so much to live for, so many changes to see."

She stretched out her legs, revealing her naked body. "They'll know. Look what he did to me!"

Adam's flashlight spilled over her body, revealing claw marks down each side of her ribs, along with a scar from a deep claw cut down the side of her neck, and bruises covered most of her body. The worst mark was the large P branding her right hip.

"He tried to mate me! Nearly four months every day. How am I supposed to go on with my life after that?"

Adam tugged his shirt out of his jeans and up over his head. He stepped next to Ty, holding out his shirt. "Here. We had no idea, Daisy."

She took the shirt, holding it in her hands as if it was a foreign object, before bringing it to her nose to smell the fresh crisp linen mixed with Adam's scent. "I haven't had clothes since he brought me here." She tugged it over her head and wrapped her arms around her body.

"Let's get you out of here. You can shower, and we'll find you fresh clothes. We'll keep you safe." Adam tried to hide the sympathy from his tone, but it was nearly impossible. If being raped by a man that kept you prisoner wasn't bad enough, add in the fact that when a shifter had sex with someone who wasn't their mate it was extremely painful. Pierce had no idea how the mating worked for shifters and in turn caused harm to Daisy.

She stood. "My Dad, do you know what happened to him?"

"No, but we'll find out. I'll get my men on it once we're somewhere safe." Ty rolled his shoulder. "Daisy, I know this isn't easy. I need to know why Pierce forced himself on you."

"He wanted a child to take over for him when the time came." She stepped off the mattress, still keeping her distance.

"Let me go first," Adam said. "There are two more shifters at the end of the hall. They're Taber's brothers, and are on our side."

Daisy glanced at Taber. "He's a bear?"

"Kodiak Bears, their sleuth is a partner of our clan. They mean you no harm. I just want you prepared when you see two large men at the end of the hallway," Adam explained, taking the lead down the hallway. Daisy walked behind him with Ty next, and Styx and Taber at the rear.

She let out a deep sigh. "I just want to get out of here and find my dad."

"There's a little motel not far from here. We'll stop to get a room so you can have a shower and change. We'll have Galen check your wounds and then we'll fly out." Ty's cell rang.

"Instead of a motel couldn't I take five minutes to shower here? I'm filthy."

They entered the end of the hallway when Ty called out from behind him. "I've got to take this call from Raja. The team can finish going through the house, but I want Adam to stay with Daisy. Have one of the other guards find her something to wear until we get to Alaska."

"Taber, you stay with Ty." Adam then turned to Daisy. "Come on, we'll find a shower for you."

Stepping past the twins, Adam holstered his gun. Soon he'd be back with Robin. Mission complete. No injuries to rack this one in the books.

Chapter Eighteen

Adam stood with Daisy, at the bottom of the plane steps, waiting for everyone to board. She wanted a moment to enjoy the fresh air on her face and the sun—a few of the everyday pleasures she had missed while being held captive. Ty stepped out of the SUV, coming toward them. "Everything okay, Ty?"

Ty dragged his fingers through his shoulder length, brown hair, tugging it out of this face. "Jinx won't be flying out with us. He'll be traveling to Ohio to meet with Korbin to act as a mediator as Korbin prepares to take over the Ohio Tigers. Once things are settled in Ohio, Jinx will return."

"Korbin?" Adam's surprise sprang from his tone. Korbin was a good guard and had the potential to make a strong leader, but he had no experience. He didn't even have the experience of working closely with the Elders. Korbin was one of the guards, but wasn't included in the Elder meetings about the clan.

"Raja's first choices wouldn't have accepted, unless you've changed your mind about leading a clan of your own?"

Adam shook his head. "No, my loyalty lies with protecting you, Tabitha, and the Alaskan clan. I want to be on the ground floor of building our future. Running a clan of my own doesn't appeal to me as much. I do appreciate you thinking that I'm ready for such a step."

"Then Korbin is our best hope." Ty gazed off to the distance.

Adam understood what Ty wasn't saying. If Korbin couldn't get the clan under control, they'd turn on him, and kill him before moving on to wreak havoc elsewhere. Even with Jinx there to consult, Korbin will have to go in strong and gain control immediately if he expects to survive. "He'll be fine."

Ty let out a heavy sigh. "If not, our only backup plan is to combine Jinx's clan with the Ohio Tigers. As it is, Jinx is going to take some of his members with him as guards to protect him and Korbin. There are only twelve members in the Ohio Tigers, but with the state of things, havoc is a strong possibility."

Jinx walked down the plane steps bag in hand, and his cowboy hat firmly in place. "I'm set."

Adam shook his head to stop from laughing. "You're going to stick out in Ohio with your cowboy hat."

"I never go anywhere without it." Jinx pulled the hat down a little further before looking back to Ty. "If anything changes and you need backup, don't hesitate to call. I'll have my plane and can be there in a matter of hours."

"Thank you, and the same goes for you. Stay safe." Ty shook Jinx's hand. "We'll see you soon."

Taber stood in the doorway of the plane. "We should be going."

"Daisy, go on in, we'll follow in a minute," Ty said. As she climbed the stairs and went inside the plane, Ty turned back to Jinx. "We need you to find out everything you can about the Ohio Tigers and a man named Randolph. He's a lone shifter. He's been seen frequently with the clan, especially with the former Alpha and Henry."

"I'll be in touch once we gather some information." Jinx nodded.

As Jinx walked to the SUV, Ty glanced to Adam. "That could have been your position."

"I know, but Alaska is my home." Adam climbed the steps to the airplane, anxious to get back to his mate. He brought the connection with Robin forward. *I'm coming home.*

Darkness had fallen on the compound hours before, but Robin couldn't sleep. She lay curled at the end of the sofa, waiting as the minutes slowly dragged. Her mate would be landing soon.

There had been so many changes in her life since Adam had found her, even more in the last forty-eight hours. The biggest was the progress she had made with Tex. He seemed calm and, more assured that nothing bad would happen as long as he was in Alaska. The abuse he suffered in Texas would always leave a lasting wound. As long as he kept it under control, it wouldn't be what controlled him. Now he was putting forth the effort to move on. Robin was glad to be a part of his journey.

If only she could have the same luck with Harmony. For now, Robin was trying to give Harmony the time she needed to adjust to the clan and for her leg to heal while they waited to find out more about Henry's whereabouts. Connor and Lukas were busy searching for his location. So far they were drawing up blanks. Robin knew they would find Henry. It would take time—time Harmony hopefully had.

"We've got Harmony settled back in her room with a guard at the door. I want you to have this." Raja handed Robin a small earpiece. "All the guards wear one. If Harmony has any other issues, the guards can contact you through this. It will also keep you informed what is happening. Understand that it's a privilege, and anything you learn should be held in strict confidence. We do not speak of Elder business to anyone outside the group without consent of an Elder."

"Thank you." Robin slipped the earpiece into her ear. It would take her time to get used to the feel and the constant chatter.

"The plane is landing in five minutes. I'm taking Tabitha to the landing strip, would you like to join us?" Raja asked.

Felix and Tabitha arrived.

"Yes, if you don't mind." Robin straightened, stretching her legs before running her fingers through her hair, fluffing her curls. Her heartbeat raced with the thought of having Adam's arms wrapped around her body again, and to feel the caresses of his lips on hers. He had been gone too long. Her body ached for his touch. She wanted to share the excitement of how much her life had changed in the short time he was gone.

As he marched down the steps of the plane, Adam was surprised to find Robin standing with Raja and Tabitha. His body called to her, his shaft instantly hardening. The tiger inside of him wanted to reclaim her as his mate, to mark her scent all over his body, and to bury his shaft deep within her warmth.

Her desires pulled him. He read her thoughts of how she wanted to run to him and wrap her arms around his body, but she waited, following the other's lead. The space between the plane and where Robin waited was only twenty feet. It felt like the longest trek of Adam's journey. Nearing Robin, he dropped his bag and wrapped her in his arms, pulling her tight against his chest. He lifted her up so he could press his lips to hers.

Her warm lips, with the hint of lingering coffee, rejuvenated him. The weariness of the trip and the tight muscles slid away. All that went through his mind was having Robin naked and beneath him. "I've missed you," he whispered against his lips.

"Oh, Adam!" She tightened her grip around his body.

Ty cleared his throat behind Adam. "Go, be with your mate. I'll brief Raja and Felix."

Adam didn't have to be told twice. He grabbed his bag and then lifted Robin into his arms. "You're mine now." He jogged away from the gathering, heading straight to his cabin.

"It took me a while to realize it, but I've always been yours." She kissed his neck. "I can walk you know?"

"We'll get to the cabin faster this way, unless you want me to take you right here."

"Inside is better." Her tongue licked down his neck, gently nibbling his collarbone.

He raced to the cabin, desperate to have her now. His tiger wasn't willing to wait any longer. Finally inside the cabin, he released her so he could open the door. Nudging her through the doorway, he growled. "I want you naked now. If those clothes aren't off you soon, I'll rip them off."

"Right to the point type of guy, I like that." She teased him and ran toward the bedroom, stripping her clothes off and let them fall to the floor in a trail of desire.

Adam slid his arm around Robin's waist, catching her before she made it to the bed. Pulling her against his body, he ran his free hand through her hair. Pressing his lips to her neck, his control was gone. His tiger wanted her hard and fast. There would be time for gentle lovemaking later, right now was about claiming his mate again. "This won't be slow."

"I don't care, as long as I have you." She pulled his shirt from his pants, her fingers teasing over his chest. "I need you, Adam."

He nodded, pushed her against the wall, and he leaned over her, claiming her lips again. He gave in to their desire, reestablishing their mating bond. His finger teased over her nipple until it was hard. Lowering his head, he drew it into his mouth and flicked his tongue over it.

"I want you naked and on the bed." Her voice was full of need as she arched her back bringing her nipple deeper in his mouth. Giving it one last

153

flick of his tongue, he let it go. He slipped his gun from its holster and placed it on the nightstand. He then unhooked his belt, letting his jeans fall to the floor.

Gliding her to the bed, he watching the way her body moved. A few scars from Bobby's abuse were visible, but didn't detract from the beauty he saw in her. A beam of moonlight from the window reflected off her silky skin.

"You're beautiful." he said. "Every single inch of you. Let me show you."

She laid back, exposing her body to him. He wanted to kiss his way from her toes to the top of her head, to show her just how much he loved her. Not tonight, he couldn't hold his beast any longer. He slid on top of her, kissing his way up from her stomach. His tongue glided over the scar on her side. A growl escaped his throat, and she tensed under him.

"What was that for?" She leaned up on her elbows, looking down at him.

"Remembering how you got his." His tongue drew lazy circles around it.

"How do you know how I got it?"

"Mates know theses things. It's a special bond between mates. However the vision of the scars origin only happens once, meaning I can touch you without seeing the images in my head again." He balanced on his arms above her. "I thought you were supposed to be lying back, letting me show you how beautiful you are." His fingers teased along the side of her body.

"We can explore later. Right now, I want you inside me."

Craving her touch, he pulled her closer, trailing a path of hot, wet kisses on her breasts, pausing to nip and suck each one. His body cried out for more of her as his hands stroked and teased until he found her special central core. His fingers delved inside her. While he worked his fingers in her heat and wetness, her body moved with the motion.

"Please, I need you," she moaned, clawing her nails into his shoulders.

"As you command, mate." He slid between her thighs and filled her with a powerful thrust. Plunging his shaft in and out of her, they found a rhythm as passion vibrated through them. She dug her fingers in his back, pulling his closer.

Robin squirmed beneath him, arching her back as her climaxed neared. She clenched her inner muscles around him, forcing him to go harder and faster. She screamed out his name as release found her. Her face shone with bliss. The warmth of her core drove him mad until his world splintered and he roared her name.

He used the last of his energy to roll to his side, cuddling against her. "I should have said this before I left...I love you, Robin Zimmer."

"Oh, Adam!" She rolled to face him. "I love you, too. While you were gone I realized you're my heart and soul."

He squeezed her tighter to his body, feeling the warmth of her next to him. "It's a dangerous time for shifters, but you have to know I'll protect you."

"I know. Will Tabitha coming out as Queen of the Tigers make the situation more dangerous?" Her fingers trailed along the muscles of his chest.

"It's likely, though the compound is safe. With the threat of Henry heading to Alaska, we've doubled the guards. All this time we thought taking out Pierce would limit the threats. Now we have other dangers to watch for."

"Hopefully we can find out where Henry is before he gets to Alaska. Harmony is having a lot of trouble, and if he was under control it would ease her worries."

Adam bent his elbow and supported his head on his hand. He glanced down at her. "You've done a lot for the clan while I was away, thank you. I hear Tex is doing remarkably well. Hopefully that will continue since we'll have to deal with the Texas Tigers soon."

"I love you, and this is your home and family, that makes everything as important to me as it is to you. I'm going to do my last semester online to get my psychology degree. I can be a licensed therapist for shifters, to help the Texas Tigers and others."

"That's wonderful, Robin. I'm damn lucky I found a mate like you." He tightened his embrace, never wanting to let her go.

The clan's safety was still in the balance, but one threat was eliminated. The Alaskan Tigers still had a fighting chance.

Until the next fight…

Preview – Trusting a Tiger

Alaskan Tigers Book Five

Felix Grady's world came crashing down around him when he received confirmation his twin brother was torturing women. One of the victims was none other than his destined mate. Torn between his twin and protecting his mate and clan, Felix must make the ultimate choice between the two.

Harmony Kirk suffered for years under her former Alpha and Henry. Now in Alaska under the protection of the Alaskan Tigers, she's expected to forget everything that happened and commit herself to the clan. Destined to be the mate of one of the top members of the clan doesn't make things any easier. It doesn't help that the destined mate is the identical twin to the man who spent years abusing her.

Will eliminating Henry make things easier or harder for Harmony? Can she move past Felix's face and see him as a different man than the one who abused her for years? Will it free her from the past she's locked herself into, allowing her to be with the man who is her destiny?

Chapter One

The sun glared down from high above when Felix Grady finally stepped out of his cabin. The day off was just what he needed. The long hours he put in while his partner Adam was off mating had worn him out. He slept late and had a leisurely lunch, but now he was tired of doing nothing. He was a tiger that enjoyed being on the move, not lounging around like a bag of lazy bones.

Taking a stroll around the compound would clear his mind before checking in with Ty and Tabitha. He knew Tabitha was in good hands with Adam, but his duties were so engrained in him that he couldn't stop, even for a few hours. It just wasn't the person he was.

Making a circle around the grounds, he checked to be sure all the guards were at their posts, nothing out of the norm. As a last-second change of plan, he turned, deciding to take a detour around the creek. Everyone seemed to love the little area by the creek. There was a little bank where shifters could relax, especially Kallie's mates Taber and Thorben who were able to fish in their bear form without anyone spotting them.

He loved the compound, and the cold weather of Alaska didn't bother him, although he didn't have nearly enough time to enjoy it. Being the Captain of Tabitha's guards takes priority, and with the constant threats to the clans, he rarely had any downtime to enjoy the compound as the other shifters did.

Raja stepped out from around a cabin. "I thought you were taking a day to relax? Checking the grounds at your normal time doesn't break from your routine. You should catch up on much deserved sleep."

Since Raja found his mate, Bethany, he had been more jubilant and full of life. The meaning of life had come back to him in full force. It was a remarkable change from the strict man that he'd been before. Now he lived for more than just his job, he had a mate that he loved. Even his sister Tora had remarked on the change.

"Can't keep me out of the action for long." He chuckled. "My tiger was restless and demanded I get back to some resemblance of my routine. Any updates?"

"Not yet. Connor and Lukas are working on finding Henry and Randolph, but no solid leads. Recently they found out Randolph spent years being Pierce's second, but he's awfully quiet so far for the death of his leader. Speaking of it, have you seen Harmony on your walk? I stopped by her studio, and she wasn't there." Raja came to stand next to Felix looking out over the creek bubbling its way down the path.

"No. I heard the guards have been taken off her door after she complained. Is that the wisest move?" There was something about Harmony that drove him to her. She was so scared and frightened, yet he could sense something hiding under the surface, drawing him to her. Maybe it was the person she used to be before his twin brother ruined the shine she had.

"You heard the stink she put up—did you want to listen to that long-term?" Raja shook his head. "Plus, we don't know when Henry might actually make his move, and we can't keep her under lock and key indefinitely. Robin will feel if she's in any danger, and we're counting on warning from you before he arrives."

"I'll do what I can." Being Henry's twin should have made it easier for him to determine Henry's next move, but he was almost as blind to it as everyone else. Harmony might be their only early warning when it came to Henry's final move.

Raja patted Felix on the back. "I better get back to Bethany. It's our night for the family dinner. Enjoy the rest of your day off."

Felix nodded, with a slight envy eating at him. His Lieutenant had a family that most of the clan was envious of. Most tiger shifter offsprings ended up leaving their home clan when they grew up to search for another one to make their name in, separating families across the country. Most shifters don't have a loyalty to a family like humans do. The loyalty was only to their mate and clan. Parents and siblings were a different category altogether for shifters. Siblings normally remained close though the distances, but parents seemed to have more of a detachment. It's believed to come from their beast since that was how they were in the wild.

Raja and Tora had been close all their lives, and Tora's mating did little to separate the siblings. What separation might have happened was closed with the birth of Tora and Marcus' daughter Scarlet. Since mating with Bethany, the family dinners have been rotated between Tora's cabin and Raja's, giving each woman a chance to host.

With family and mating on his mind, he decided to extend his walk down the creek bed before going back to check on Tabitha. The lush trees lined the creek, keeping it hidden even from the cabins. It was a safe and secure spot deep within the compound, one you were never sure who you would find there.

A familiar scent of honeysuckle and toasted vanilla teased him further along the path to one of the hiding spaces that Kallie favored when she first came to the clan. There, hidden amongst the trees, Harmony sat with her back pressed against the base of one of the trees, tossing rocks at the creek.

"Harmony." He called to her before stepping closer because he didn't want to scare her. He knew that just the sight of him made her tense, serving as a reminder of the man that forced himself on her. It was still hard for him to believe that his twin had done such an unimaginable thing. They were raised better than that, and having the tiger inside him but being unable to shift was not enough of an excuse for Felix to forgive Henry's behavior.

She slid her legs up tight against her chest and met his gaze, but she didn't speak. She watched him like a tiger stalking its prey, but she wasn't strong enough to take him down. In tiger form, he outweighed her by more than a hundred pounds, but even as a human, she was no match for him. His years of training and hours in the gym meant he could take her down without hurting her and without much effort at all.

"You okay?" He stepped closer, keeping in her line of sight and his hand way from the gun in his shoulder holster.

"I can't take it any longer." She leaned her head against the tree and looked at him. "I can't stand the fear, the panic. Damn it, to be a prisoner, it's like being with him all over again. I keep waiting for him to find me, to make me pay for running."

"You're safe here. He's not going to get to you. I won't let him. Do you understand that?" He knelt in front of her, just far enough away that they didn't touch, still respecting her space.

"You can't be sure of that. There are so many threats against your clan now, with the Texas Tigers and the rogues." Her jaw was set as she stared at him. He could read it in her body language that she didn't believe him.

"I told you I'll protect you, and I will. There are always threats to clans, but that doesn't change my vow to protect you." He paused, listening to the quietness, when an idea struck him. "I know you're feeling boxed in, so how about if we take a drive? There's no need to go into town or anything, but a drive through the area might help you recharge and get outside of the compound for a bit. What do you say?"

"I don't know."

He could feel her hesitation. "If we're going to live together in the same clan, you'll need to move past your apprehension of me. I understand why you have it, but I can't change my looks or what Henry did to you. I also know words don't mean much, but I'm nothing like he is. Let me prove it. There's somewhere I want to show you." He stood. "What do you say?"

She nodded. "Okay. To get out of here, even just for a short time, would be heavenly."

He smiled at her. "I need to swing by to see Tabitha and get the keys for one of the guards' SUVs then we can go. Ten minutes."

She stood and brushed off the butt of her jeans. "Should I meet you somewhere then or something?"

"Come along—it's fine. I'm off-duty today, but I want to check in with Adam." He led the way up the creek a bit further until they came to a small footbridge to cross back over. There were so many things he wanted to ask her, but he didn't. Spooking her would only send her back into her retreat, and it took too long to get her out of her tigress form to risk anything that might send her back. He'd wait until she was ready.

Silence fell over them like a warm blanket. The only thing heard was the crunch of the occasional stick under his boots. There were no birds that frequented the area—too many tigers and bears in the area that scared them off. Felix always enjoyed the quiet, but now in the quiet he found his thoughts full of the woman standing next to him.

"Hey, Felix," Tabitha called to him as they stepped out of the trees.

"Tabitha and Adam, just the people I was on my way to see. What are you doing out here?" Felix quickly scanned the grounds, checking for any threat.

"Robin's down with a cold and asked me to check on Harmony," Adam explained.

"I hope Robin is all right." The common cold was not something Felix or the other shifters had to deal with, only their human counterparts. Once a shifter went through the change, they couldn't catch a cold or the flu, which came in quite handy. Even though Robin was human, she would gain a higher tolerance to illness from her mating, making illness uncommon. The Alpha/clan bond between Robin and Harmony was highly unusual, especially considering Robin was human, but it was there. Robin had no idea how to handle the connection as a shifter automatically did, so it was becoming a learning process for her. In the meantime, the connection was draining her to the point of illness.

"Bethany healed her, so she should be back to normal soon." Tabitha nodded.

Felix accompanied Robin on her daily visits with Harmony a few times a week, trying to get her used to his presence. Robin was working closely with Harmony to get her to open up and to work past what Henry put her through.

"I was going to take Harmony out for a drive. She's suffering with a little cabin fever, and I thought a little time off the grounds would give us both a break." He almost asked if they would like to join, but instead he kept it to himself. It wasn't for Harmony's sake but because he wanted to be with her without the others gathered around. He felt the need to prove to her that he was nothing like Henry.

Harmony wasn't the first woman to see him as a threat or to fear him, and in most cases, that's what he needed. With Tabitha's security on the line, he had to seem like a bastard that would do what he threatened. His threat should come from his actions and body language not necessarily from words. However, when it came to Harmony, he was going out of his way to see that she didn't fear him. *Why?*

Trees whipped past the SUV window as Harmony and Felix headed further and further away from the compound. Her heart beat frantically against her ribs, her mind racing through her fears. She could taste her pulse in her throat. What if this was a trap? He could be leading her to Henry. After all, they were twins—surely they had some bond.

"You're going to have Robin calling." Felix never turned his gaze away from the road.

"What?"

"Your fear. If I can feel it this strongly, I wouldn't be surprised if Robin calls and orders me to return you to the compound at once." He looked over at her. "Maybe this wasn't such a good idea. Do you want me to take you back?"

Part of her wanted to scream 'yes,' but if he were taking her to Henry would he have offered to take her back to the compound? She didn't think so. More importantly, Robin trusted Felix, therefore she was trying to. He might look like the man who had raped and tortured her for months, leaving scars all over her body, but from what she saw of him, he was different.

Staying in Alaska close to Robin, the only person she had any loyalties to, she'd have to trust Felix and the other clan members. This was the first step on the long road to the life she once had. Not that she ever thought she'd be the person she once was. "No, I want to go."

"I know you're scared. I should have asked someone else to come, but with Robin a little under the weather, I was out of people you trusted. We could do this another day when Robin can come with us."

Pawing at her jeans, she tried to wipe the sweat that had coated her palms away. "It's fine. I wanted to get out. You know Adam wouldn't have wanted Robin to leave the security of the compound without him, and you both couldn't have left Tabitha unguarded."

"Then Adam could take you and Robin, and I will stay at the compound."

"No." She turned away from the window to look at him. "Felix, I want to trust you, and I'm trying."

"I understand. Every time you look at me, it's hard for you to see me as someone other than Henry. It's going to be over soon."

Hadn't she heard that since she arrived at the compound? It had been weeks of sitting around waiting for Henry to either attack or for someone to find him. In all that time, her leg nearly healed from the nasty bear trap wound. She was tired of waiting—if only she could do something about it. Even if Henry couldn't shift, he had proven more than once she was no match for him.

"There's a slight difference in your features. Your jawbone is a little more rounded, the dimples are a little deeper, and your eyes are different. They still hold the edge of danger, but there's a touch of understand and friendliness to them. The biggest difference between you two is your attitude. He's, well…"

"Insane?" he supplied.

"Yes." She shrugged. It was awful to say it aloud, but it was the truth. "I'm sorry."

"There's no need to apologize. It's true, and I've known it for years. When we turned eighteen, our parents moved to Australia so they didn't have to deal with it any longer. The tiger inside him has driven him crazy from not being able to shift. The only difference between Henry and a rogue is that rogues are put down when the tiger takes over. Looks like Henry's fate will be finding him at last." Felix turned the SUV onto a dirt road, doing his best to avoid the potholes.

She felt her eyes narrow down at him, watching him intently. "Even though he's your brother, you'll kill him?"

He slid the SUV into Park and looked at her. "Yes. Brother or not, he can't do what he's done and get away with it. There's no other recourse for what he's done." He let out a deep sigh. "Years ago, when the tiger first started to drive him toward madness, I wanted to do it then, before he could cause any problems. It might seem heartless to some, but we're not like humans. There's not a hospital we can put him in. It's what our kind does when one is sick, we put them out of their misery. Henry is driven by his madness. He's no longer the brother I grew up with."

Without thinking, she reached across the gap and laid her hand on his lap. It's what their kind did when someone hurt. Touch gave them comfort. Her fingers brushed against the back of his hand, and unexpected electricity shot through her. "*No!*" Tears welled in her eyes with the knowledge of what that meant. *Oh, shit—it can't be!*

Marissa Dobson

Born and raised in the Pittsburgh, Pennsylvania area, Marissa Dobson now resides about an hour from Washington, D.C. She's a lady who likes to keep busy, and is always busy doing something. With two different college degrees, she believes you're never done learning.

Being the first daughter to an avid reader, this gave her the advantage of learning to read at a young age. Since learning to read she has always had her nose in a book. It wasn't until she was a teenager that she started writing down the stories she came up with.

Marissa is blessed with a wonderful supportive husband, Thomas. He's her other half and allows her to stay home and pursue her writing. He puts up with all her quirks and listens to her brainstorm in the middle of the night.

Her writing buddy Pup Cameron, a cocker spaniel, is always around to listen to her bounce ideas off him. He might not be able to answer, but he's helpful in his own ways.

She loves to hear from readers so send her an email at marissa@marissadobson.com or visit her online at http://www.marissadobson.com.

Other Books by Marissa Dobson

Alaskan Tigers:

Tiger Time

The Tiger's Heart

Tigress for Two

Night with a Tiger

Trusting a Tiger

Alaskan Tigers Box Set Vol. 1

Jinx's Mate

Two for Protection

Bearing Secrets

Tiger Tracks

Healing the Clan

Alaskan Tigers Box Set Vol. 2

Her Black Tiger

Tiger Trouble

Alpha Claimed

Forever Creek Shifters:

Forever's Fight

Protecting Forever

Stormkin:

Storm Queen

Crimson Hollow:

Romancing the Fox

Loving the Bears

A Lion's Chance

Swift Move

Purrable Lion

Bearly Alive

Saved by a Lion

Furever Mated Box Set

Reaper:

A Touch of Death

SEALed for You:

Ace in the Hole

Explosive Passion

Operation Family

Marine for You:

Lucky Chance

Back from Hell

A Marine's Second Chance

Tanner Cycles:

Until Sydney

Phantom Security:

Different Sides

Undercover Agent

Cedar Grove Medical:

Hope's Toy Chest

Destiny's Wish

Leena's Dream

Fate:

Snowy Fate

Sarah's Fate

Mason's Fate

As Fate Would Have It

Half Moon Harbor Resort:

Learning to Live

Learning What Love Is

Her Cowboy's Heart

Half Moon Harbor Resort Vol. 1

United Homefront Ranch:

Destination Heaven

Beyond Monogamy:

Theirs to Treasure

Clearwater:

Winterbloom

Unexpected Forever

Losing to Win

Christmas Countdown

The Surrogate

Clearwater Romance Volume One

Small Town Doctor

Stand Alone:

Through Smoke

SEALed Rescue

SEALed in Texas

Starting Over

Secret Valentine

Restoring Love

Made in the USA
Coppell, TX
26 November 2019